TOUCHED BY
GRACE

USA TODAY BESTSELLING AUTHOR
ALICIA RADES

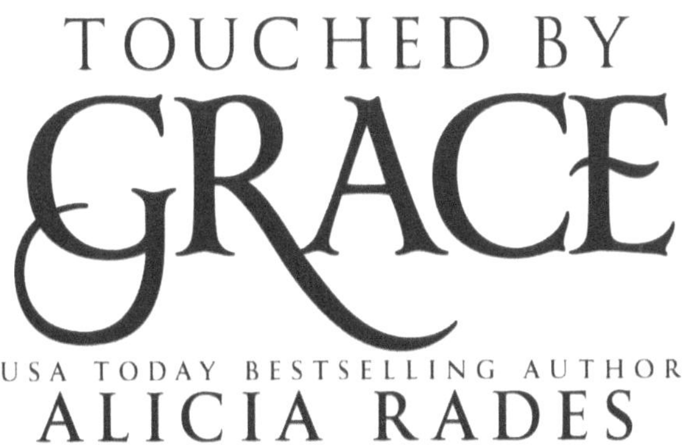

Published by Crystallite Publishing.
Produced in the United States of America.
Edited by Megan Linski.
Proofread by Emerald Barnes.
Cover design by Rebecca Frank.

To my family.

Flying through the sky in the midst of a raging thunderstorm was *not* how I pictured my first day at Galen High. Mrs. Anders called this a training exercise; I called it insanity.

Rain pounded down hard on my wings. I had to work ten times harder than normal to lift them and stay airborne. My soaked clothes weighed me down, and wet hair stuck to the side of my face. The frequent wind gusts weren't any help, either. My shoulders ached. I wasn't sure how much longer I could keep this up, but I'd be damned if I admitted defeat on my first day.

A hill rose ahead of me.

Only a lap and a half left.

The task was simple. Fly from one end of the valley to the other and back. Repeat five times. It reminded me of the grueling pacer tests I took at my old schools. Only this time, there was lightning.

Thunder cracked above me when I reached the far end

of the valley and turned. Just when I thought it couldn't get any worse, the skies opened wider. I could hardly see through the thick downpour. My classmates had disappeared from view.

I pushed forward faster, flapping my wings as hard as I could. I hadn't been flying my whole life like everyone else in class had, but I *wasn't* going to be the last one back.

A wind gust rushed by me, throwing me off balance. My body lurched several feet to the left. In a moment of panic, my heart felt like it was falling out of my chest. I quickly steadied myself, but I couldn't tell if I was still on the right flight path.

I blinked away the rain and squinted ahead of me. Water continued to rush across my face, obscuring my view.

Lovely. Mrs. Anders was trying to kill me. Too bad she didn't realize my death would cause the end of the world.

Without warning, a blonde figure burst through the rain and slammed straight into me. Casey's screech filled my ears as we spiraled out of the sky. My legs twisted under me when we landed, and pain shot through my ankle. Casey fell on top of me. I gasped for breath as rain continued to beat down on us.

Blonde Bitch groaned and pushed herself to her feet. "Are you crazy, Ryn? If we were flying any higher, you'd have gotten us both killed!"

Air finally returned to my lungs. I rolled onto my stomach to keep from inhaling the rain.

"I couldn't see anything," I defended. "This whole exercise is suicide!"

Mrs. Anders swooped out of the sky and landed beside us. Her tall, muscular frame towered above me. Apparently *she* wasn't having any problem seeing through the rain. She'd been standing at the top of the valley with a damn umbrella watching us try to kill ourselves.

"What was *that?*" Mrs. Anders demanded. Her voice rose to be heard over the wind. "Didn't I emphasize at the beginning of class how important it was to stay in your own lane?"

Maybe she should've had us flying laps instead of sprinting in imaginary *lanes*.

Several students who'd already finished landed behind her to see what was going on. I didn't know most of them, but I recognized one of the guys who always hung out with Casey. I still wasn't sure if his name was Troy or Trenton.

I pushed myself to my feet. I tried not to put too much pressure on my right foot. "I'm fine, thanks for asking."

It wasn't exactly true. I was pretty sure I'd sprained my ankle from the fall.

"I'm glad to hear that," Mrs. Anders said. She didn't sound like she meant it. "But maybe we should have you sit out until you've had a little more practice."

I could hear it in her voice. She was *so* not pleased with having a total noob in her class.

I crossed my arms. "Or maybe *you* shouldn't run drills like this in the middle of a freaking storm!"

I realized what I'd said a moment too late. I'd never talked back to a teacher like that before. But who could blame me when rain was pounding down on us like this?

Mrs. Anders's brows shot up. "Are you trying to tell me how to run my class?"

Detention, here I come.

"No, I just—" I started, but Mrs. Anders cut me off.

"If you want to become a Protector, you're going to have to learn how to fight in even the most difficult circumstances."

The thing was, I wasn't sure I *did* want to become a Protector. Celebrity chef still sounded like a good job title, but that wasn't exactly Davina-specific.

"You never know when you'll have to fight a demon," she continued. "It could happen in the middle of a storm like this. I suggest you pay attention in your strategy class."

Didn't she realize this was literally my first day?

"Thanks, I'll be sure to do that," I said flatly.

Mrs. Anders stared down at my foot and frowned. She must've noticed I wasn't putting any weight on it.

She turned to Casey. "Miss Harris, would you please escort Miss Tyler back to school? Have Mrs. Banks check on her ankle."

Casey huffed. "Fine."

I limped along beside her as we headed toward the wooden stairs built into the tall hill. Casey reluctantly wrapped an arm under my shoulder to help steady me. I suspected she was only helping to get out of the rain.

We entered the forest along the trail that led back to school. The thick tree cover helped shelter us from the bulk of the rain, but the wind continued to rush through the trees.

"Is Mrs. Anders always like that?" I asked.

"Yeah, she's kind of a hardass," Casey answered.

"I take it she doesn't like new students."

"She doesn't like *incompetent* students," Casey emphasized.

Clearly she had some harsh feelings about being knocked out of the sky. That, or there was another reason she hated me. Namely, the hottest guy on two wheels in our class.

I had half a mind to tell Casey just how wrong she was about my incompetence, about how I'd killed five demons at once. But Fletcher didn't want anyone to know I had the Power of Grace. He didn't seem to trust all the Davina in town, and he certainly didn't want the demons hearing about it. Otherwise, I'd have more than just the *one* who wanted my head. Instead of telling everyone what really went down a week ago, Fletcher told them he'd taken care of Dorian himself.

Dorian. The thought of him twisted my stomach.

Casey and I hobbled across the school grounds. Galen High—or Galen Mansion, as I thought of it—towered three stories above us. We entered through the back door. Water squished through my tennis shoes and trailed behind us as Casey led me to the cafeteria.

I pulled a heavy mahogany chair out from the closest table and sank into it. Without a word, Casey turned from me and disappeared behind a swinging door that led to the kitchen. I took a deep breath and began wringing my hair out onto the hardwood floor. I shivered.

My eyes scanned the cafeteria. Four long rows of dark antique-looking tables spanned the length of the room.

Each was lined with ten chairs on both sides. A large serving window was cut out between the kitchen and the cafeteria in the corner of the room. This place looked more like a reception hall than a high school cafeteria.

Casey returned shortly with a red-headed lady wearing a hair net.

"Hi, I'm Mrs. Banks," she introduced herself.

I returned her smile. "I'm Ryn."

"And I need to go change." Casey turned on her heel and left the room.

Mrs. Banks pulled out a chair and gestured for me to lift my ankle. She peeled back my wet jeans and inspected it while she spoke. "I'm sorry we don't keep a nurse on staff, so you're stuck with me. But don't worry; I have a background in medicine."

"Why doesn't Galen have a school nurse?" I asked.

"There aren't enough students for it to make sense," Mrs. Banks answered. "Out of the eighty kids who attend, we maybe have two or three a year who require medical attention."

She pressed on my ankle in search of tender spots. Luckily, there didn't seem to be too much damage.

"I think I'll be fine," I said. "Can I get some ice?"

"Sure." Mrs. Banks gently set my ankle down and stood.

Just as she disappeared into the kitchen, Fletcher walked by the cafeteria doors. He stopped when he noticed me. Fletcher wore his usual tan slacks and button-down shirt. He'd rolled up the sleeves, which looked strangely casual on him. It wasn't exactly the type of look I expected to see on a sixty-something-year-old guy.

He stepped into the room. "Are you okay, Ryn?"

I pushed my wet hair out of my face and smile reassuringly. "Everything's fine. I've just been introduced to Mrs. Anders's flying class. She's a lovely woman."

Fletcher smirked. "I take it things didn't go well?"

"Nah. I only fell a mile out of the sky and twisted my ankle."

Fletcher raised his eyebrows. "A whole mile, huh?"

I held back a laugh and nodded.

Mrs. Banks returned with an ice pack and a towel to mop up the wet floor beneath me.

"Can I borrow that?" I asked as soon as she was done.

She handed me the towel.

I used it to dry my hair out. Too bad I didn't bring extra clothes. I wasn't looking forward to walking around in wet underwear all day.

Allie should've warned me.

I handed the towel back and looked at Fletcher. "Why aren't you in class?"

"It's my prep period," he stated. "I was working on copying some papers. Since you have some free time, why don't you stop by my classroom once you get cleaned up? There's something I'd like to discuss with you."

It sounded like bad news. This had to be the worst first day of school ever, and I wasn't even a full hour into it.

I thanked Mrs. Banks and then hurried to the bathroom. I pushed through the door just as Casey was making her way out. She'd changed into dry clothes and brushed out her hair. She breezed past me without saying a word.

I sighed and turned to the hand dryer on the wall. I did

the best I could drying out my hair and shoes, but my jeans still stuck to my legs like packaging tape.

I turned to the wide mirror above the sink. My eye makeup had been smeared from the rain, and the cute curls I'd put my hair in this morning were now flat. I ran my fingers through my hair to help with the tangles, but it didn't help. Even the pretty purple dangly earrings I'd put in this morning couldn't help improve my disheveled appearance.

I eventually gave up and headed down the hall to Fletcher's classroom.

"Miss Tyler," he greeted. He stood from his desk and grabbed a large roll of paper the size of a baseball bat.

I sank into one of the desks at the front of the room and pressed the icepack to my ankle. "What am I in trouble for?"

Fletcher furrowed his brow. "You're not in trouble. I just wanted to give you this." He unrolled the paper across my desk.

I scanned it for several seconds before realizing it was a map of Eagle Valley.

I looked up at him. "What do I need this for?"

"I thought if you had a visual, you might have an easier time pinpointing Grace's location," he said.

I sighed heavily. *Grace*, the ancient Davina who remained our only hope for defeating the Aedes. For reasons that still baffled me—and probably everyone else— it was up to *me* to awaken her. I just had to find her first.

I could hear Fletcher's voice in my mind. *You were chosen by Grace. Her magic will lead you to her.*

He'd said that to me two weeks ago. According to him, some sort of divine fate had brought me here. Apparently that was proof Grace was nearby.

I wasn't sure I believed him. But maybe this map would inspire me.

I could only hope, because if something didn't happen soon, the Davina would be facing the end of the world alone. And I wasn't sure we'd win.

2

Itook the time I had before second period to drop the map off in my locker outside Fletcher's classroom. The modern lockers looked strange in contrast with the older architecture of the mansion.

The bell rang while I stood at my locker double checking my schedule for the day. The hall filled with students. Several people stared at me as they passed, no doubt wondering about the new girl.

I noticed Allie immediately. She seemed well within her comfort zone, shooting smiles and waving at people as she passed. She hadn't held back on the makeup today. Her eyes were outlined in black, and she'd twisted her dark hair into a cute updo with loose tendrils framing her face.

Allie's face fell when she saw me. I probably looked like a drowned rat.

"A little warning would've been nice," I said light-heartedly.

Allie leaned against her locker beside mine. "I'm so sorry. You must've had Mrs. Anders first period."

I ran my fingers through my damp hair. "That obvious?"

She nodded. "Don't feel bad. I totally forgot a change of clothes. I have her later today."

I kept my schedule in my hand and shut my locker. "What'd you have first period?"

"Magical defense."

I scanned the schedule I'd received this morning. "I don't see that class on here."

Allie's brows drew together. She stood beside me to inspect my schedule. "Maybe Fletcher got you out of it. You know, because…"

Because I still wasn't great at controlling whether or not my magic would stun or kill. And we didn't want to accidentally reveal I had the Power of Grace. That's why Fletcher and Marek had been training me in private.

"You have Fletcher next period with me," Allie said. "That's our mentor group. That class is a little different. They like to mix up the grades for training so we can mentor the younger ones."

I barely heard the last half of what she said as my gaze locked on Marek. His brown hair stood up in the front like he'd put effort into styling it that way. He strolled down the hall with his hands tucked casually in the pockets of those tight jeans I liked. He'd ditched his leather jacket and wore a light blue t-shirt that matched his eyes. A confident smile touched his lips like he was happy to be back at Galen High after a long summer.

I had the strongest desire to kiss those lips.

It'd been nearly two weeks since our first kiss. Since then, I hadn't gotten so much as a peck from him. The guy hadn't even *held my hand* in days. Sure, he had a thing for saving my life, but apparently kissing me more than once would be too much to show he cared.

It wasn't like we didn't spend time together. In fact, we'd spent every day training together since the kiss. I'd been practicing how to fly and learning how to conjure fireballs. Though, in Marek's words, *they're not fireballs.*

He smiled at me as he entered Fletcher's classroom.

That's it?

I had half a mind to call Marek out on his behavior right then and there. I scowled and followed behind Allie into the room.

Fletcher gestured to the desks in front of us. "We don't have assigned seats. You can sit anywhere you'd like."

I returned to the seat at the front of the room where I'd left my icepack. Marek sat on my right while Allie took the desk to my left. Two terrified freshman boys had claimed the desks farthest from the door.

"Hey," Marek said with a sympathetic smile.

I ran my fingers through my hair nervously. "Hi."

Marek glanced down at the icepack. "Are you okay?"

"Just a mishap in flying class," I answered.

Kyle found his way into the room a minute later, followed closely by two girls I didn't know. He sat next to Allie. An uncomfortable silence hung in the air. It was cut only by the sound of the bell.

A young boy rushed into the room and shyly took a seat next to the other freshmen. "Sorry I'm late," he breathed.

"Not to worry." Fletcher stood from his desk. "To some of you, welcome back. To the others, welcome to Galen High."

The freshman boys sank in their seats with wide eyes, looking positively terrified.

"I'm your mentor, Fletcher. This class gives you the chance to hone your skills and improve in any areas you might be struggling in. We all work together to help each other reach their full potential. You may come to me at any time with questions. Now, take a look around you."

My eyes scanned the room and met several other gazes.

"This is your team," Fletcher explained. "We're here to lift each other up and learn how to fight together. This is the team you'll be with for battles. At times, we will be divided based on skill level."

Wonderful, I thought. *He's going to place me with the freshmen.*

"For example," he continued. "The upperclassmen have their first battle next week during the last period of the day. Obviously, we don't want the freshmen going up against other upperclassmen so soon, so your first battle will be in about a month."

One of the freshman boy's eyes widened.

"Don't worry," Fletcher assured him. "You'll start out up against people of your own skill level. We don't have any juniors in our group this year, so the sophomores—" he gestured to the two girls I didn't know "—will have a chance to battle with the seniors."

Fletcher turned to the whiteboard behind his desk and popped the cap off a black marker. "First things first. Let's hear some suggestions for this year's team name."

"We're sticking with the Saints," Kyle said, like he'd made the decision for the whole group.

Fletcher wrote *Saints* across the board. "Any other suggestions?"

"I like Saints," the red-headed sophomore said.

"We've always been the Saints," Marek pointed out. "I say we keep it."

Fletcher turned from the board. "This is an entirely new team this year, but if everyone is in agreement, we can recycle the name from last year's team."

The freshman boys seemed too afraid to say anything. The rest of us agreed to call our team the Saints.

Silence fell over the room. I took the opportunity to raise my hand nervously.

"Yes, Ryn?" Fletcher called on me.

"Yeah, I have a few questions. First, what are the battles?"

Fletcher leaned against his desk. "Good question. They're mock battles. Your team will go up against another team of students to practice your skills in a real-life setting. You'll be able to use your wings, your magic, or your hand-to-hand skills. There are a few variations. Sometimes you're allowed to stun, and the last team standing wins. Other times, stunning is off limits, and you'll have to rely on your combat skills to beat the other team."

My jaw dropped. "Don't people get hurt?"

"It wouldn't be fun if nobody got hurt," Kyle said with a smile.

A boy gasped from behind me.

"Where do you think this came from?" Kyle gestured to his slightly crooked nose. "Started healing before we could set it."

"The battles are supervised, and there are rules," Fletcher clarified. "You have nothing to worry about. The accident Kyle's referring to took place during an unscheduled and unsupervised training session, and he didn't seek medical attention as he should have."

Kyle smirked and shot Marek a glance like they shared some sort of inside joke.

"The battles are like football," Kyle said. "Sure, someone's bound to get hurt once in a while. But instead of playing other schools, we play against other Davina."

"So, it's like a sport? A game?" I asked.

"Yes," Fletcher answered. "Each win earns you points."

One of the freshman boys shot his hand into the air.

"Logan?" Fletcher called on him.

Logan spoke softly. "Do we have to participate?"

A sympathetic expression fell over Fletcher's face. "I will not *force* anyone to do anything they don't want to do, but I will point out that the purpose of Galen High is to prepare you to become a Protector. You're going to have to know how to fight. Unless you'd rather be working in Galen High School's kitchens as soon as you graduate."

Yes, please! Where do I sign up?

He raised his brows like that would be the worst thing in the world. "One day, perhaps sooner than you think, you'll be up against the Aedes. As Davina, it's our duty to protect the earth. We do that one Aedes at a time."

Another boy raised his hand.

"Yes, Ethan?" Fletcher said.

"My mom says that fighting the demons is pointless. That there are so many of them that the Protectors will never be able to keep up."

Fletcher raised his brows. "Yes, there are a lot of Aedes, but—"

The final boy cut in. "My parents say being a Protector is super dangerous, that you're just as likely to kill a demon as they are to kill you."

A shiver ran down my spine at the thought.

The room broke into whispers. The three freshman boys leaned together to discuss all the rumors they'd heard. Kyle hissed something in Allie's ear about how dumb the freshmen were.

Marek leaned over to me. "Don't worry. That's what your training's for."

"Calm down," Fletcher commanded.

The room went silent.

"Yes, there are a lot of Aedes out there," Fletcher said. "But how many do you think there would be if there *weren't* Protectors minimizing the threat? As for fighting them, there's a chance they'll kill you first, just like in any war."

Chatter began its way around the room again.

"Why are we even fighting them?" Ethan asked, sounding genuinely curious.

Fletcher tilted his head like he couldn't understand why

anyone would ask such a question. "Because, Ethan, they feed off human essence. We fight them because this is our world, too. If we don't strike first, the Aedes will wipe us out. Then they'll get the humans to destroy each other. We may not have the numbers to eliminate every threat, but we will certainly do what we can."

Ethan raised his hand again and began speaking before Fletcher could call on him. "Doesn't legend say the portals to the demon realm could open back up one day?"

My breath stopped.

Fletcher answered calmly, but I sensed a hint of fear in his expression. "It's always a possibility, Ethan, but so is the chance that the Davina realm will open again as well. If such a thing *did* happen, you'd want to be prepared, wouldn't you?"

Fletcher's eyes connected with mine for only a split second. I still managed to catch his silent message.

Time was running out, and I wasn't prepared yet.

3

"Did you see the look Fletcher gave you?" Allie asked after second period.

Even after all the questions that filled the last half hour of class, I still couldn't get that look out of my head.

"You noticed?" I asked.

Marek stopped beside us. "How's that coming, by the way?"

"What do you mean?" I opened my locker and placed the warm icepack inside.

Kyle leaned against the locker next to mine. "We all saw the look. Fletcher's obviously curious how things are coming along."

"They're not really coming along at all," I admitted. "I need more training. Maybe there's more to my powers than I've discovered so far." I paused. "Or *maybe* he could be a little more helpful than handing me a map and hoping I'll be able to point at a spot and solve all our problems."

"I'm sure he doesn't expect that of you," Allie said kindly.

I resisted the urge to roll my eyes and tell her just how much it felt like it.

"We'll figure it out," Marek said with certainty.

He was so close in the crowded hall that I could feel the warmth radiating off him. I wished he would pull me into his arms.

"What's your next class?" he asked.

"Physical combat," I told him.

"Me, too. Let's walk together." That was all it took to make me feel ten times better.

"Kyle and I are in that class, too," Allie said.

The four of us walked upstairs together. We entered a small classroom that mirrored Fletcher's and sat in the back corner.

My stomach dropped when Blonde Bitch entered the room and took the seat in front of me. She didn't even look like she'd been flying through a rain storm earlier today. I noticed a couple of other students from first period had also cleaned up.

A dark-skinned man who looked to be in his fifties stood at the front of the room. His blue polo shirt must've had slits in the back for his wings since they rose out of his back.

My class schedule told me his name was Mr. Collins.

"Calm down, everyone." Mr. Collins rose his voice over the thick chatter.

The room quieted.

"Unfortunately with the rain," he said, "we're going to be having class inside today."

"Upstairs?" one of the guys across the room asked.

Mr. Collins shook his head. "No. Today, we'll cover this year's curriculum."

I shot Allie a questioning look. "Upstairs?"

She leaned over and whispered to me. "We sometimes train on the third floor when it's too cold outside."

"Quiet please," Mr. Collins said sternly.

I looked to the front of the room to see he was staring straight at me.

"You must be Kathryn Tyler, our new student."

"Uh, yeah. Call me Ryn."

"Why don't you come up and introduce yourself?"

Ugh. I was hoping I wouldn't have to do this.

I tried not to limp on my sore ankle as I stood from my desk and walked to the front of the room. The class was small—with maybe only a dozen people—but it didn't make me any more eager to introduce myself.

I faced the class. "Hi. I'm Ryn. I just moved here."

There. That should satisfy him. It's not like there's much else to say.

"Which school are you transferring from?" Mr. Collins asked.

I opened my mouth to answer, but then I realized he wasn't talking about just any school.

"This is my first time at a Davina school," I said.

He frowned. "And they put you in my combat class? Do you have any experience?"

Were all the teachers at this school asshats?

"I took martial arts as a kid." Not that I remembered a whole lot from it, but I knew how to block a punch.

Mr. Collins pressed his lips together like he wasn't impressed. When he didn't say more, I returned to my seat. It looked like I was going to have to work extra hard to get my teachers to like me.

Casey's eyes followed me all the way back to my desk. She scoffed and tossed her hair over her shoulder as she returned her attention back to the front of the room. She didn't seem to notice her hair spilling onto the top of my desk.

I gritted my teeth in annoyance. *She's probably trying to mark her scent all over me as a way to get to Marek.* I narrowed my eyes at the back of her head. It was because she realized she had competition, and not just in the romance department. I certainly had a shot at beating her in a battle. *Maybe.*

"If looks could kill..." Allie mused on our way to the cafeteria after our fourth period battle strategy class.

"What?" I honestly had no idea what she was talking about.

Allie smirked. "I saw you throwing daggers at the back of Casey's head in physical combat."

"I'm obligated to hate her," I pointed out. "I'm your friend, and you despise her."

I didn't mention there were other reasons I wasn't fond of Casey. I worried she still liked Marek. But that whole thing apparently happened way back in freshman year. Casey should've moved on by now.

Besides, Marek would never go for her anyway, I told myself.

My second inner voice quickly countered. *Then why doesn't he seem interested in you lately?*

I ignored the voices battling it out in my head. Instead, I focused on the smell of burgers and tatertots wafting from the cafeteria. In the lunch line, Mrs. Banks winked and slipped me a few extra tots. So far, that was the highlight of my day.

Allie led me to a table in the far corner of the lunchroom, where Marek and Kyle joined us shortly after.

"Hey, Ryn," Marek kept his voice low. "I was thinking about what you were saying earlier."

I swallowed my food quickly. "About what?"

"About Fletcher expecting you to point to a spot on the map he gave you."

"And?" I raised my eyebrows.

"I think you might be on to something. Maybe try the dart thing," he suggested. "It worked for you before."

Allie tilted her head in question.

"It's what brought me here," I explained to her. "Mom let me choose where we were moving this time. I left it up to fate by tacking a map to the wall and throwing a dart at it. Landed right on top of Eagle Valley."

Maybe Marek was right and fate would lead me to Grace again.

Allie's eyes widened. "You really think that'll work?"

I shrugged. "Doesn't hurt to try. Want to come over after school? We'll see if we can find Grace."

4

"$\mathcal{W}$as it terrible?" Allie asked on our way home from school.

"Was what terrible?" I tore my gaze from the gray sky and looked at her from where I sat in the passenger seat. My backpack and the map sat in my lap.

"Your first day," she said. "Was it as bad as you thought it'd be?"

"Not too bad," I lied. My jeans were still damp from this morning. "I'm used to being the new kid. Except, I think people seemed a little more interested in me than normal."

I swear every person I walked past had to stare at me.

"It's because it's a tiny school," Allie said with a shrug. "What else are people going to be interested in? Besides, you're pretty. It makes you more interesting."

I batted my eyes at her. "You think so?"

She laughed.

I quickly composed myself. "In reality, they were only

staring because I look like I just crawled from the depths of Malum."

Allie shot me a shocked expression.

"Sorry," I said regrettably. "Was that offensive? I just meant—"

"No," Allie interrupted. "I just didn't expect you to make a Davina joke."

I relaxed.

"And you were worried you wouldn't fit in," she teased.

"I wasn't worried." *Okay, maybe a little bit.*

I quickly changed the subject. "Is it just me, or did it seem like Fletcher was ignoring me during history?"

Allie pulled into her driveway. "He wasn't ignoring you. He was teaching. He has, like, two totally different personalities. One minute, he's in mentor mode; the next, he's in teacher mode. It's like somewhere between second and sixth period he turns into a completely different person. Don't take it personally."

"I'll try not to," I said, stepping out of the car.

Allie and I crossed her lawn onto mine and headed up my porch steps.

"How was school?" Mom called when we entered the house.

I poked my head into the living room. "It was good. Lots of homework. Allie and I are going upstairs to work on it."

Mom looked up from the scarf she was crocheting. "Okay. Don't forget about your chores."

I turned so she wouldn't see me roll my eyes.

Upstairs, I dropped my bag at the foot of my bed and unrolled the map across the mattress.

"Feel anything?" Allie asked hopefully.

I shook my head. I couldn't believe Fletcher actually thought this might work.

"Maybe we should start in our history book," I suggested. "There might be a clue about Grace in there."

Allie looked uncertain. "Wouldn't someone have found her already if there was?"

My shoulders dropped. "I guess so."

"I like Marek's idea," Allie said with a shrug. "You made it to Eagle Valley. You've come this far already."

And there was still no guarantee Grace was here. It was only a theory.

I sighed. "Okay."

I turned to my dresser and opened the top drawer. I rummaged around through the junk and found two stray pushpins. I used them to tack the poster-sized map to the wall.

I turned to my closet and felt around in the darkness for my pile of shoeboxes.

"Here," I said, handing Allie a shoebox. "Check to see if there are any darts in there."

Allie sat on my bed and pulled the top off the box. "I thought you said you'd unpacked everything."

My voice became muffled as I stuck my head deeper into my closet. "I did. I just keep a few boxes of junk that never get unpacked. There's no point in it."

"Then why do you keep this stuff?"

"I figure it might come in handy at some point. Like

this." I drew away from the closet and held up a dart in triumph. "You ready?"

Allie set her shoebox aside. "You betcha."

I stood across the room and angled myself toward the map. Nerves fluttered in my gut when I drew my arm back, closed my eyes, and hurled the dart toward the wall. I heard it land softly—not a noise I was expecting.

I slowly peeled my eyes open. Confusion hit when I saw the map remained dart-free. The dart never made it that far. Instead, it stuck straight into my carpet.

Allie burst into laughter and rolled herself onto the bed like she couldn't control herself.

"Maybe... you should keep... your eyes open," she suggested between laughs.

Maybe you should bite me.

I snatched the dart up from the ground. "I wasn't trying to *aim*."

She composed herself enough to sit back up. "Well, at least aim for the *map*."

I sighed and turned back to face the wall. Keeping my eyes open this time, I locked my gaze on the map, not focusing on any area in particular. This time, when the dart flew from my fingers, it hit the wall with a satisfying *thud*.

"Yes!" I cried in victory.

Allie and I hurried over to the map to see where it hit. It landed near the center atop a small, clear section of grass.

I let out a breath in annoyance. "Great. According to this, we'll find Grace in the middle of nowhere."

Allie leaned closer to the map. "No, that's the park. We should check it out."

I plopped down on my bed. "I'm not sure I feel fate guiding me on this one."

"It's worth a shot," she said. "Would you rather sit here reading our history book or be out there taking action?"

When she put it that way, the answer was obvious.

Action, it was.

5

"I told you this would be useless," I said to Allie on our third walk around the park. "All that's here are some trees and a playground."

"There are a couple of buildings," Allie pointed out.

I glanced around and inhaled the scent of rain that still hung in the air. "Are you suggesting Grace is living in one of the toilets? Because I don't think the bathrooms or the pavilion have been here that long."

Allie spun slowly in a circle, gazing out into the distance. "Maybe we're missing something. Maybe there *was* a building here when the town was settled. Or *maybe* she's buried somewhere beneath our feet."

"Don't you think there'd be a marker? Like a gravestone or something?"

Allie shrugged. "I don't know. Maybe one of these trees marks the spot they left her. Or maybe you were a little off when you threw the dart. She *could* be in the cemetery.

That must've been around as long as the town has been here."

"Where's that at?" I asked.

"Just over there." Allie pointed past the playground. "On the other side of those trees."

I sighed heavily. "I don't know. I honestly just feel like going home. We could give our history book a shot, and—"

"Heads up!"

Allie and I jumped out of the way just in time as a Frisbee flew by our heads.

"Holy crap!" Allie cried, holding a hand over her heart. "Are you *trying* to decapitate us, Trenton?"

I recognized the guy jogging toward us. He was the bigger of the two guys who always hung out with Casey, the one in my flying class. Finally, I could match a name to the face.

Trenton pushed wavy blond hair from his eyes and bent to pick up his Frisbee. He shot Allie a sly smile. "So what if I was? Doesn't hurt to scare the competition a little, does it? I hear we're going up against you next week for our first battle."

Allie dropped her hand from her chest. "We're not trying to *kill* each other. Sometimes I think you guys take this competition thing way too seriously. One day, we'll be fighting alongside each other. You know that."

"Relax," Trenton said. "I was only joking. It's Casey who's serious about the competition. You know how she is."

Allie scrunched up her nose like she knew *far* too well.

Trenton turned to me and stuck his hand out. "Hi, I'm Trenton. Ryn, is it?"

I nodded and took his hand. He had a strong grip.

"I hear you've been flying well this past week." A slight smile touched his lips.

Allie's brows shot up. "From who? Casey? I find it hard to believe Casey would give such a compliment to someone other than herself."

"You really hate her, don't you?" Trenton asked, amused. "Actually, Troy was telling me."

I blushed slightly, thinking back to a few days ago when I'd been training with Marek and didn't realize I had an audience. By the time I landed, several groups had entered the valley. I remembered Casey and Troy being among the crowd.

"It's nice of him to notice," I said. "Why haven't you been showing up with Casey and Troy to practice?"

"I've been out of town visiting family," Trenton explained.

Allie glanced around. "Where's your team now?"

"Um… not sure. We don't spend every waking second together."

It seemed like they did. I rarely saw Casey without being followed by her two bodyguards.

Trenton smiled. "It's just me, playing a round of Frisbee golf. Any chance you want to join me? I have a few extra discs in the car."

I was surprised at how kind Trenton seemed without Casey around. I was just about to accept his offer when Allie answered for me.

"Actually, we're kind of busy," she lied. "We have to get home to work on our homework."

Trenton spread his arms wide. "On the first day of school? Blow it off. You'll still graduate."

A little part of me wanted to agree with him.

"Come on, Ryn," Trenton encouraged, nudging me with his elbow. "Don't be afraid of me just because I hang out with Casey." He stared down at me and smiled sweetly.

"I guess we could play *one* game," I heard myself say.

Trenton's smile grew. "Great. I'll go grab my extra discs." He hurried toward his car while Allie and I walked slowly toward the first disc golf platform.

"What are you *doing*?" she hissed.

"I don't know. I figured it wouldn't hurt to have more Davina friends. We might compete during mock battles, but like you said, we're not enemies."

"Yeah, but he's *hitting* on you."

"No, he's not," I insisted.

"He complimented your flying. Plus, did you *see* the way he looked at you?"

"You mean guys can't compliment me without flirting? And I don't think he looked at me in any special way."

"Okay, maybe he wasn't *hitting* on you, but he's definitely acting strange," she said. "It's usually all trash talk with Casey's group."

"Maybe he's different when he's not around her," I pointed out.

"Maybe," Allie agreed with a hint of skepticism in her voice.

Allie and I stopped at the platform and waited for Trenton to return with his discs.

Allie went first. Her disc flew in an arc and ricocheted off a tree. It landed in a mud puddle fifteen yards away. I held back a laugh.

Allie turned to me. She didn't look amused in the slightest. "Let's see *you* do better."

I stepped to the front of the platform and swung my arm around, flicking my wrist at the last second. My disc flew gracefully through the air and landed halfway to the basket. I smiled at her and stepped aside for Trenton.

He drew his arm back for an underhand swing. "Let me show you ladies how it's done."

His strong arm swung around, and his disc flew above the grass with speed and precision I couldn't imagine myself having. The disc landed mere yards from the basket.

My eyebrows shot up. I was impressed.

The game continued like that for the next hour. It turned out I wasn't half bad at Frisbee golf. I wasn't as good as Trenton, but I beat Allie by fifteen points.

"You know," Allie said on our ride back home from the park. "We never checked out the cemetery."

"Sorry," I said. "I didn't mean to get sidetracked. We don't really have time tonight. My mom's going to be on my case as it is since I ran off before doing my chores. We'll check out the cemetery another time."

"Yeah," Allie said slowly, not taking her eyes off the road. "I just hope we figure all this out soon."

6

woke with dread the following day. Rain gently tapped against my window, which meant another day of torture in first period. I packed my backpack with a change of clothes and extra makeup. Luckily, by the time Allie and I made it to school, the rain had let up. Unfortunately, that didn't make Mrs. Anders's flying class any easier.

We met her at the top of the valley. Below, several groups of students threw white fireballs at foam targets. Another group watched their mentor demonstrate how to block punches.

My jaw dropped in awe. It was like the entire valley had transformed into a training arena since I'd last seen it. Before school started, it was peaceful and quiet. Marek and I almost always had the place to ourselves. Now, it seemed crowded. The extra training equipment scattered around the vast field beneath us only took up more space. My eyes darted between each group of students, trying to take in the wonder of seeing so many Davina in action.

I didn't have long to observe the scene before Mrs. Anders blew her whistle and called us to attention.

Today's exercise involved performing flips in the sky like we were freaking gymnasts. It was supposed to help us learn how to correct our flight if we were ever attacked while airborne. As far as I was concerned, she could shove her whistle and this entire training exercise where the sun don't shine.

Mrs. Anders blew her whistle and yelled at me at least six times. I was sure she'd like nothing more than for me to sulk back to the school and demand to drop her class.

But I didn't.

I was, however, relieved when first period ended.

In second period, Fletcher led our group of nine back out to the valley. He turned to us when we emerged from the forest. "Settle down."

The sophomore girls giggled next to each other, and the three freshman boys whispered amongst themselves. Marek and Kyle had been talking, too, but I didn't catch what they were saying. It took several moments before everyone went silent.

"Today, I will be assessing your skills." Fletcher spoke loudly. "We'll do this several times throughout the year to see how you've improved and to identify which areas our team needs to work on. I want Ethan, Logan, and Dylan to start with conjuring essence. Allie and Kyle, I'd like your help with them."

I could only pray for whichever kid ended up with Allie

as their teacher. She was a great friend, but she hadn't exactly been much help when teaching me how to conjure fireballs.

"Emily and Ruby—" he gestured to the two sophomore girls "—you can start on targets. You know the drill. Marek, I want you to help Ryn on her hand-to-hand skills."

Everyone split off in their own directions.

"Why don't *I* get to practice with targets?" I asked Marek as he led me to a clear stretch of grass out of the way of the other Davina.

"Your essence still shines purple sometimes," Marek reminded me. "We don't want to risk anyone seeing that. We'll practice on our own after school."

"Allie and I have plans today," I told him.

Marek frowned. "We already missed practicing yesterday."

I held my hands up. "No need to throw a temper tantrum. I need time to search for Grace. Or would you rather I spend all my time training with you?"

The answer was obvious; I had to be out there doing *something* to find Grace. But I had this strange desire to hear him say he'd rather spend time with me.

"Okay, tomorrow then," Marek decided. "We'll need to find somewhere else to train, though. The valley's not private enough now that school started. We had a few close calls last week."

"James Marek," I teased, "are you asking me out on a date?"

I could only hope he'd say yes.

"No," he answered too quickly.

My heart dropped. I'd only been joking; I didn't expect the rejection to hit me that hard. Stupid overactive hormones.

Marek leaned into me and spoke softly. "If I took you on a date, it'd be special. Not the same training we've been doing."

And just like that, my heart lifted to settle back in its proper place in my chest.

I elbowed him lightly. "I was only joking, but if the offer for a date ever *is* on the table, I'll take you up on it." I grinned widely.

Apparently, I wasn't being obvious enough, because Marek didn't say another word on the date front. He *had* to know I was into him. We'd kissed! Or maybe that was the problem. Maybe he didn't like the kiss. Maybe he didn't feel the same chemistry I did. Maybe—

Marek's arm swung out and caught my left shoulder.

"What the hell?" I cried, holding onto my arm. I knew he was going easy on me, but dammit, that *hurt*. "I wasn't ready."

"That's the idea," he said with a smile.

And that smile was all it took for my mind to fall back into daydreaming about him. The damn boy was distracting as all hell.

He swung another fist at me. I ducked and then immediately aimed a foot at his abdomen. We weren't trying to hurt each other, but I didn't think it mattered how hard I kicked him. It still felt like kicking a stone wall.

"Good job," Marek encouraged, circling me like he'd felt

nothing. "But you'll have to do better if you're going to stand a chance against a demon."

"Give me a break."

Marek raised his brows. "And what happens if a demon attacks you tomorrow? He's not going to give you any breaks."

I held my palm up and wiggled my fingers. "That's why I should be working on my magic. He wouldn't stand a chance."

"Neither would you if an army of demons found out what you were," Marek pointed out.

"Might I remind you that already happened? And I killed them."

Marek hesitated a moment then continued circling me. "You almost killed yourself, too."

He had me there.

Marek jabbed another fist in my direction. I instinctively threw my arm out to block him. His fist cracked into the side of my arm painfully. He had no idea how strong he was.

Almost instantly, his other hand came flying at my head. I jumped backward and put several feet of space between us so he couldn't reach me.

"Impressed yet?" I asked smugly.

"I'm going easy on you," he asserted.

"Sure you are." I rolled my eyes.

Before I knew what was happening, Marek lunged at me. He grabbed my body and whipped me around so that my back was pressed to his front. He pinned both of my arms to my chest. My breaths became shallow, and my heart raced. He breathed in my ear, and for a moment, I thought I might collapse. My knees simply didn't want to hold me up anymore. Every inch of my body heated. He *had* to feel the energy sizzling between us.

"What was that you were saying?" he whispered.

I swallowed, wanting nothing more than for him to hold me in this position forever. Surely by now he could feel my heart trying to beat its way out of my chest.

"I—I don't remember," I said breathlessly.

He laughed lightly. "How are you going to get your way out of this one?"

I twisted my head around to look him in the eyes. My gaze drifted down to his lips, then back up to his eyes. Kissing him would certainly get me out of it.

The sound of a fireball connecting with a target nearby snapped me out of my trance.

"Like this." I threw my hips to the side and wrapped my leg behind him.

He toppled backward onto the grass and released me on the descent. Shock crossed his face, but it only lasted a split second. A smile formed.

He propped himself up on his elbows. "I wasn't expecting that. What's your next move, Ryn?"

I don't know. Straddle you and kiss every inch of your body.

"Um… run away?"

Marek's brows shot up. "So that your opponent can stun you from behind, giving him enough time to kill you?"

I threw my hands up. "I don't know, Marek. Even if I did get on top of you to pin you down, it wouldn't matter how strong I am. I don't weigh enough. You'd just toss me off of you." I paused. "I guess my next move would be to stun you, to immobilize you so I could…" I didn't like how that sentence ended.

"Good," he said.

I offered my hand to help Marek to his feet.

Practice continued for another forty-five minutes. By the time Fletcher told us to head back up to the school, my shirt was soaked in sweat. Stepping back into the air conditioned building was a relief.

"Feel free to talk amongst yourselves until the bell rings," Fletcher said when we returned to his classroom. "Ryn, can I see you at my desk for a moment?"

Nerves knotted in my gut as I made my way to the front of the room. Did he think I did poorly during practice today? Was he going to assign me a different partner because he noticed how distracted I became around Marek?

"What's up?" I asked in a shaky voice once I reached him.

He spoke quietly so no one else could hear. "I wanted to make sure you were okay and not feeling too over-whelmed. I fear you might think I'm expecting too much of you."

The way he said it made it sound like he heard my friends and me talking in the hall the previous day.

I shifted my weight between my feet uncomfortably. "Well, the weight of the world is kind of resting on my shoulders at the moment. Honestly, as my mentor, I thought you'd be more helpful."

I was surprised to hear the words come out of my

mouth. I tried not to, but I could be a real asshole sometimes.

"I'm sorry you feel that way," Fletcher said. "See that stack of books there?" He pointed to a pile of books beside his desk. The stack came up to my knee.

I nodded.

"Those are the books I've been looking through to see if I've missed something. I'm hoping there might be a clue somewhere about Grace."

It was official. I *was* an asshole.

And Fletcher was acting all calm like I hadn't just accused him of being totally worthless.

"I'm sorry," I said in a small voice.

Fletcher looked at me seriously. "While I'm going through these books, you might start by talking to Elizabeth Ellington. She's the librarian at the public library here in town. She's quite knowledgeable about the town's history."

I bit my lip. "I thought you were the Davina history expert."

Fletcher nodded lightly. "On ancient Davina history. Elizabeth knows more about the town's history. If my theory is correct and Grace was brought here with the Davina who settled the town, we might be able to find something in the town's records."

"Yeah, I suppose…"

Fletcher stared up at me like he expected me to say more.

"I'll go talk to her after school," I finally said.

That seemed to be all Fletcher wanted to talk about. Without another word, I returned to my seat.

"What was that about?" Allie asked under her breath.

"Change of plans. We're headed to the library after school."

"Okay," she said. "Hopefully we'll find something useful."

I pressed my lips together in uncertainty. "Yeah. Hopefully."

7

"How can I help you?" a woman behind the library's front desk asked as Allie and I approached. She looked about sixty, but her hair had only begun graying. She'd piled it atop her head in a loose bun, and she wore thin black reading glasses.

"Hi," I said. "We're looking for Elizabeth Ellington."

The woman smiled brightly and removed her glasses. "I am she."

"Hi. I'm Ryn, and this is Allie. We're writing a paper for our history class. Our teacher said you might be able to help. The paper's on the history of Eagle Valley."

"Which school do you ladies go to?" Elizabeth asked.

"Galen High," Allie and I answered in unison.

Elizabeth stood and leaned over the front desk. Her eyes darted from side to side to make sure no one was listening. She whispered softly. "So, you're looking for information about *Davina* history?"

"Yes," I answered eagerly.

She held up an index finger. "Give me one moment, please."

Elizabeth walked to a door behind the front desk and stuck her head inside. I could just barely make out what she was saying. "I have some students here I'm going to be helping out. Do you mind keeping an eye on the front desk for me?"

While we waited for her, my eyes scanned the room. It wasn't a large library by any means, but it was beautiful. An area outlined in a rug and several antique-style chairs stood behind us. I could picture myself relaxing in one of those chairs with a good book and never get sick of it.

Above us, the ceiling rose to the second level, where a balcony framed the room. Tall wooden bookshelves reached the ceiling on both levels. Between them, natural light flooded in from high windows. The place reminded me of an old church.

Elizabeth's quiet voice pulled my attention back to her. "Follow me, please."

She led us down a large staircase at the front of the building. The basement air was cool, and the hall was lined in thick stone. Elizabeth stopped at a door near the end of the hall. Her keys jingled in her hands.

"This is our archives room." She pushed the door open and flipped on the light.

We entered a room the size of Fletcher's classroom. Rows of bookshelves lined the walls, and an empty table stood in the center.

"We don't typically let students in here due to the delicacy of the documents, but I like to make exceptions for

Galen High students." She gave a sweet smile. "You'll find most of the early history in this section." She pointed. "It's mostly newspapers, unfortunately. Have a seat, and I'll see if I can find some good articles for you ladies to use on your paper."

Allie and I both sat at the table.

"Are there any books that mention the Davina in Eagle Valley?" I asked.

Elizabeth disappeared down one of the rows. "I'm afraid there aren't any specific to Eagle Valley. You'd have to look in your school library for books on Davina history. There aren't many written texts left on the Davina."

"Why not?" I asked.

She poked her head out past the row of shelves and glanced at me above her glasses. "Many of the stories have been lost, unfortunately. Why do you think no one knows about the Davina anymore? They all worship their own gods and goddesses." Her voice became muffled as she returned down the row. "It's better that way, to be honest. Then we don't have people actively seeking us out. Can you imagine what it would be like in this day and age? We'd all be captured for science experiments!"

I looked to Allie. "Why were the stories lost in the first place?"

"I thought they taught you that in your history class," Elizabeth said.

"She's new at Galen," Allie explained before turning to me. "After Praesid put the Originals under protection, people started to question if they were truly still around. Generations passed. Since humans couldn't see the demons, some groups stopped believing they were out there. When the Originals didn't return, they made up their own stories."

"And the Davina let everyone believe whatever they wanted?" I asked.

Allie nodded. "The fewer people who believed in the Davina, the safer the Originals were."

"Here's a good one." Elizabeth returned a moment later and set an old newspaper in front of us. "Be careful with it. The article is on the second page. It explains some of the town's history."

Allie gently unfolded the newspaper and began scanning the pages.

Elizabeth disappeared down the row again. "Many Davina stories are handed down generation by generation the good old way—through oral storytelling." She laughed lightly. "Don't tell anyone I said that. I'm a librarian. I'm supposed to love books."

Elizabeth came back carrying another stack of newspapers. She sat across from us. "What is it exactly that you want to know about the Davina?"

Where they left Grace. If she's still here after all this time.

"Nothing... in particular," I said slowly. "Our paper is going to focus on landmarks and buildings that were here early on. We'd like to give a picture of what the town looked like when it was settled." I hoped that lie would be enough to help us narrow down where Grace might be hidden. "Were there any significant landmarks built at the time? Especially any that could be tied to the Davina?"

"It's all tied to the Davina, so I'm not sure what you mean," Elizabeth said.

All I knew was that if Grace was as important as she seemed, her grave would be marked somehow. Then again, Praesid had been protecting her. They wouldn't make it that obvious.

"I'm not sure what I mean, either," I admitted sheepishly.

Elizabeth turned to Allie. "Did you find anything in that article you can use for your paper?"

"Um… yeah," Allie said, but I heard the lie in her voice. Clearly she didn't think any of it would be useful on our search for Grace. "It says the town was settled in 1857 by a group of men who came from out East and purchased the land with gold earned from their family business."

"That would be the three Haylo brothers," Elizabeth said. "They were Davina."

"Right." Allie glanced back down at the article. "They settled the area for farmland, but once the railroad hit the town, the community expanded."

Elizabeth nodded. "And at that time, it was mostly Davina. The people closest to the Haylo brothers prior to their purchase of the land were the ones who came to settle the town first."

"The article doesn't say much more," Allie said. "It lists which businesses cropped up first."

I immediately perked up. That information could be useful if they'd hidden Grace inside one of the businesses.

"Which ones?" I asked, almost too quickly.

"Um…" Allie bit her lip and scanned the page. "It says

there was a blacksmith shop, a grain mill, a lumber yard, and a few department stores."

None of those sounded like plausible candidates.

"What about things like churches?" I asked. If an angel was hiding anywhere, that was as good of place as any to start.

Elizabeth laughed from across the table. "Are you forgetting that the town was settled by *Davina*?"

"So?" I glanced between her and Allie.

They both gave me strange looks.

"The Davina don't associate themselves with any modern religion," Elizabeth explained. "Some Davina communities used to build churches as a way to blend in. Eagle Valley didn't get its first church until thirty years after the Haylo brothers bought the land. That was shortly after others began moving into the town. You know, people who weren't Davina."

I nodded. So, what did we have? A list of a few old businesses that probably didn't even exist anymore?

"What about other places that *weren't* businesses?" I asked. "Things like government buildings?"

Elizabeth's face lit up. "You're standing in one! This library was among one of the first buildings built by the settlers. It was originally both the library and the town hall, but after they built the new town hall in the thirties, the library expanded to the entire building. And then there was the Haylo brothers' mansion, which of course is now Galen High School."

My heart surged with hope. Why hadn't I thought of that before? Better yet, why didn't *Fletcher* think of that?

It made so much sense. The Davina had retained control of the building for so long. Grace would still be protected, even if no one knew they were protecting her.

"Other than that," Elizabeth said, "the only things I can think of that would've been around in the earliest days of Eagle Valley are the cemetery and a couple of houses."

Right. The cemetery. Allie and I still had to check that one out. Now at least we had two other ideas to add to the list: the library and the school.

"Thank you, Mrs. Ellington," I said with a smile. "You've been a huge help. Can we take any of these newspapers to help with our research?"

Her expression dropped. "I'm sorry, but unfortunately, we can't allow these out of the library. You're free to take any notes you wish, and you can take pictures so long as the flash is turned off. If you don't have any more questions for me, I'll let you girls browse the newspapers alone."

She glanced at her watch. "Please let me know when you're done so I can close the room back up. I'll be at the front desk."

Allie's eyes followed Elizabeth. "Thank you. You've been so much help already."

"No problem, girls," Elizabeth said as she left the room.

Allie turned to me immediately. "Anything jumping out at you yet?"

"I think we definitely need to check out the library and the school."

"After the cemetery, though," Allie insisted. "Your dart landed right next to the cemetery, so I think that has to count for something. We'll go tomorrow when we have more daylight to explore. I don't think we'll have time today once we're done here."

"Okay," I agreed.

Allie reached over to grab half the stack of newspapers in front of us. "I'll take this half."

I slid the second half in front of me.

Allie pulled out her phone and snapped a picture of the article she'd been reading. I thought it was a good idea, so I set my phone on the table beside me.

I sighed heavily and unfolded my first newspaper. I could only hope we weren't missing something important.

Several hours later, Allie and I gave up reading the newspapers as it neared closing time. We returned upstairs to tell Elizabeth we were finished and that she could lock the room back up.

When I turned from the counter to leave, I was surprised to see a guy sitting in one of the chairs with his head buried in a book. The sight of Trenton reading made him seem ten times hotter. His eyes darted up from his book for just a moment, and they met mine. He snapped the book shut and set it aside before getting to his feet.

Allie didn't seem to notice his approach until he spoke.

"Hey, ladies." He fell into step beside us.

Allie shot him a suspicious glance.

"Hey, Trenton," I said.

The three of us stepped outside into cool air and stopped on the landing before the steps. The sun had already fallen low in the sky.

Trenton leaned against the concrete banister. "What are you up to?"

"None of your business," Allie said.

No need to be so harsh, I thought.

"We were just researching," I told him, hoping it would make up for Allie's rudeness.

"Oh?" he asked with raised eyebrows. "Researching what?"

"It's for a school project," I told him quickly.

"Yeah, me too," he said flatly.

What school project did *he* have?

"What are you up to now?" he asked.

"Nothing, really," Allie said slowly. "You're being weird again."

Trenton rolled his eyes. "Maybe I'm trying to make up for all the shit Casey's put you through. You don't have to hate me just because I hang out with her."

Trenton had a point. Personally, I had no problem with him, but Allie still had reservations.

She opened her mouth, but nothing came out. When she couldn't come up with a rebuttal, her shoulders relaxed. "Okay, but do you really want to hang out with *us*?"

Trenton glanced around. "I don't see anyone else to hang out with."

"So we're just the most convenient option at the moment?" Allie asked.

I nudged her with my elbow. She didn't have to be so rude.

Trenton smiled. "Basically, yeah. I'm bored. So sue me."

"Don't listen to Allie," I insisted. "It's her time of the month."

Allie let out a breath of air, but I ignored her.

"What did you have in mind?" I asked.

Trenton shrugged. "Anyone up for flying?"

My heart soared at the thought of flying, and I quickly agreed.

Several minutes later, Allie and I rode to the school in her car while Trenton took his own vehicle.

"I think Trenton must like you," Allie said to me on the way there.

"I don't really get that vibe," I told her, though I had to admit the idea flattered me.

"He seems pretty eager to hang out with you," she pointed out.

I shrugged. "I think he's just bored, like he said. It must get exhausting to hang out with Casey all the time. He's probably just looking for a change of pace."

"Yeah, maybe," she agreed when she pulled into the parking lot.

I was glad I'd continued wearing tank tops even when I wasn't sure if I'd be flying that day. It made impromptu flying sessions like this so much easier. I took a mental note to get Mom to order me more tanks online. Which meant I actually had to do my chores and get on her good side.

"Trenton is *so* going down," Allie muttered to me on our way toward the valley. She eyed him from where he walked several paces in front of us.

"Don't be so mean to him," I insisted. *He's not Casey.*

"I wasn't trying to be. He just… has all that muscle, and…"

"Are you checking him out?" I teased.

"What?" She sounded shocked. "No, I just meant… he thinks he's so great because he's strong and all, but I'm a fast flyer. I can beat him."

I tried to hold back a smile. "I can't wait to see you try."

Allie held her chin out proudly. "Watch me."

When we reached the valley, it was completely deserted apart from the training equipment that'd been left out.

Trenton spread his arms out and circled to look back at us. "Check that out. We've got the place all to ourselves."

He reached for the bottom of his shirt and pulled it up over his head. I knew the guy was muscular, but *damn*. I thought for sure I even saw Allie checking him out. He could definitely give Marek a run for his money.

Trenton flexed his shoulders, and white wings sprouted from his back. I'd found that every Davina had a slightly different shade to their feathers. Allie's shimmered a subtle blue, while mine held a hint of purple in them. Trenton's wings, I was surprised to see, had a duller hue. Even in the dimming evening light, they didn't shimmer quite the same way mine and Allie's did.

"What are we doing? Racing?" Allie asked.

"What else?" Trenton replied.

Without warning, they both sprinted to the edge of the hill and threw themselves into the air, spreading their wings wide. I quickly followed behind, digging my feet into the ground and springing upward. My wings spread out behind me. I laughed in exhilaration as I flapped them and flew higher.

Up here, high above the valley, I could almost forget about my troubles. All my cares slipped out the window, like Grace didn't matter anymore.

As I expected, I came in last place. I was so far behind that I couldn't even use their head start as an excuse. Allie had done as she'd promised and beat Trenton. The way she talked about him, I expected him to be a sore loser, but he only smiled and challenged her to a rematch.

The three of us raced several more times. Each time, Allie won and I lost. I eventually grew so tired of flying that I sat in the grass to cool down. My wings spread out behind me.

"You okay?" Trenton took a seat beside me. He leaned back on one hand and rested the other elbow on his knee.

"I'm fine. You guys can keep racing."

"No, it's cool," he told me. "Allie's made her point. Clearly she's a better flyer than me. Always has been."

Allie blushed before she launched herself back into the sky for another flight.

"What about you?" Trenton asked.

"What *about* me?"

"What are your special talents?" He smiled encouragingly.

"Um…" I dropped my gaze and fidgeted with the red stud in my ear.

It might've sounded like I was trying to be modest, but the truth was that I had to think about the question. I didn't really have hobbies. For the first time in my life, this Davina stuff actually felt like something I could stick with, and not just because I felt obligated to. There was a thrill that came along with flying and conjuring essence that I couldn't quite explain. I only wished I'd discovered it sooner.

"Really?" Trenton asked. "Nothing?"

"Sorry," I said. "I don't really have an answer. I'm still new to all this."

"That doesn't mean you're not special."

Well, I *was*, in a way, but I wasn't about to tell him that.

"Thanks." Blood rushed to my cheeks. I did my best to avoid his gaze. Instead, my eyes locked on Allie as she flew around the valley. In the dimming light, it was hard to make her out the farther she flew away from us.

"So," Trenton said after a short silence, "what brought you to Eagle Valley?"

The first time I told Marek it was fate, I'd only been joking around. Now that I'd decided fate actually had something to do with it, it didn't feel right to mention it. Not when Trenton didn't know I had the Power of Grace.

"What brings anyone to Eagle Valley?" I said vaguely, purposely not answering his question.

"Usually family."

I couldn't exactly use that as an excuse. I really should've thought my answer through. It was always one of the first questions people asked when I moved to a new town. I was surprised that Trenton had been the first person to bring it up all week.

I settled with the basic explanation. "My mom likes to move around. I was born in the Midwest not too far from here, and I always loved the area. I convinced her to come back. I just got lucky that I ended up in a town with Davina." I paused momentarily. "What about you? Didn't Casey say you started at Galen sophomore year?"

Trenton nodded. "Like I said, family."

Allie landed a moment later and fell to the grass beside me, exhausted.

"Enjoying yourself?" I asked.

"Yeah," she breathed heavily. "Anyone up for another go?"

Trenton and I both declined.

"It's getting late anyway." I stood and pulled my wings into me. "Mom's going to be mad because the library closed and I'm not home yet."

"Okay." Trenton sounded disappointed. "Maybe we can hang out another time."

"Yeah," I agreed. "You ready to go, Allie?"

She took another deep breath and pushed herself up. Her wings disappeared behind her. "Yeah."

"See you later, Trenton," I said with a wave. I turned to Allie on the way back to the car. "See? He's not so bad, is he?"

Allie's lips turned down. "No, I guess not. Just be careful, okay?"

"What do you mean?" I asked.

"Don't lead Trenton on. I don't think Marek would be thrilled to have competition."

I let out a breath of disbelief. Maybe Marek *needed* competition. He wasn't exactly fighting for my affection lately. Trenton actually seemed like he cared.

I think I'd very much like to see what Marek thought of me spending time with Trenton.

9

"You know Trenton?" I asked Marek after school the next day.

Dumb question. Of course he knows Trenton.

The halls had been deserted, leaving Marek and me alone at our lockers. It was my first chance to talk with him alone all day.

"Yeah," Marek answered.

"We hung out yesterday," I stated.

"And?" Marek asked.

That was it? No hesitation? No demanding to know where we'd been and what we'd done? Marek was acting like an entirely different person than the guy I knew.

"And…" I started.

Say you care. Say you're jealous. Say something!

This wasn't how I expected this conversation to go.

"I was wondering what you thought of him," I said.

Marek's features hardened. He shrugged. "He's an okay

guy, I guess. But you really shouldn't be hanging out with people when you should be focusing on Grace."

Now he was bossing me around? What the hell?

"*We're* hanging out right now," I pointed out.

"So we can train," Marek said. "If we can get you more in tune with Grace's essence, you might have an easier time finding her. And Fletcher says you'll need to be in control of your essence to wake her."

"I know," I said with a sigh.

"Should we get started?"

Marek's idea of a private place to practice was in Fletcher's classroom.

Fletcher sat behind his desk, watching my every move. He said he was reading through his stack of history books looking for clues about Grace, but I could feel his eyes on me the whole time.

"Okay." Marek clapped his hands together. "Let's see what you've got."

I held my hand out nervously. I took a deep breath and channeled my energy down my arm. I felt my skin heat as a white orb formed in my hand. I smiled at how effortless it looked, but the moment I let my guard down, the orb darkened to purple.

I closed my palm instantly. "Shit. I'm going to end up killing someone, aren't I?"

So far my uncontrolled essence had only killed demons. Luckily.

Marek placed a careful hand on my outstretched fist. Good thing I didn't still have a fireball in my hand. If my essence reacted the way my heart did, it'd go flying across the room.

"You're not going to kill anyone," Marek promised. "That's why we're getting you to practice. Can you see now why we didn't have you practicing out in the open?"

"Yeah," I said begrudgingly.

"Try it again," Marek instructed. "Concentrate this time."

"I was concentrating."

I focused harder on keeping my magic a crisp white. When I glanced up to Marek's face, his sexy stare distracted me again. The orb flashed purple.

"Damn." I dropped my hand. "What am I doing wrong?"

Marek pressed his lips together. "I'll be honest. I'm not sure. I think it might be a matter of concentration."

Then it's definitely not going to work with you around.

"We just have to find what works for you," Marek told me. "Two weeks ago you couldn't conjure essence by will. Then you realized what it took for you to do it. Suddenly, it wasn't so hard."

"You mean when I realized I could only do it if I was protecting someone?"

"Exactly."

I shrugged uncertainly. "I don't think that's going to help. If I'm protecting someone, my essence is going to turn deadly."

At least, that's what my track record showed.

"I didn't mean that's what's going to help you control your essence," Marek said. "I just meant that we have to find what *does*."

I gritted my teeth. "I'm trying, you know."

"I know." Somehow, Marek kept calm as my frustrations grew. It only made me want him more.

"Try conjuring your purple essence first," Fletcher suggested.

I turned to face him. "What?"

"You're having trouble sustaining white essence," Fletcher said. "Try starting with purple essence to see if that's easier."

I bit my lower lip. "Okay."

I took a deep breath and held my palm out again, this time focusing on the higher charged, electric essence that flowed through me. I wasn't sure how I could tell the difference between the two. It was almost like flexing a separate muscle.

A purple fireball formed. I stared at it intensely, concentrating to maintain the purple hue. I feared it might turn white any second. It didn't.

Marek's voice broke my concentration a minute later. "Great job. What do you say we try the other hand?"

"What?"

"So far you've only practiced with your right hand," he pointed out. "Let's see what your left can do."

I couldn't hold a spoon with my left hand. What made him think I could handle a fireball with it?

"It's okay," Marek encouraged. "You can do it."

I held out my left palm and concentrated on channeling my magic down my arm. My brows constricted, and my jaw clenched. Nothing happened.

"Calm down." Marek gently placed a hand on my shoulder.

I forced myself to listen to him, but it took another fifteen minutes before a purple fireball finally formed.

I jumped in excitement. "I did it!"

"Great." A huge smile formed across Marek's face. "Do it again."

My excitement quickly fizzled.

I tried again, this time succeeding within the first five minutes of trying. Unfortunately, Fletcher's room wasn't big enough to practice much more than that. Another hour and a half passed before we finally called it a day. I pulled out my phone and texted Allie to let her know I was done. Marek said goodbye and slipped out of the room.

"Can I have a word with you, Ryn?" Fletcher asked before I left.

I met him at his desk.

"Did you find the map useful?" he asked.

I dropped my gaze. "I kind of had a feeling about the park, but Allie and I didn't find anything there."

That was a lie. It hadn't exactly been a *feeling*.

Fletcher nodded in thought. "Have you talked to your mother about any of this?"

"No," I answered automatically. "Why would I?"

Even if she *did* believe it, she'd be pissed I'd been lying to her all these years about seeing the demons.

"She doesn't know anything," I insisted.

"That doesn't mean she doesn't deserve to know," Fletcher said. "She may be human, but she's still your mother."

I pursed my lips. Who did he think he was, telling me how to navigate my relationship with my mom?

"With all due respect, Fletcher, I know my mom better than you do. She wouldn't want to hear about any of this."

Fletcher stared at me in shock. "I'd certainly want to know what was going on with my kids—especially if they were in your situation."

I crossed my arms. "You mean being the chosen one? Being hunted by demons for what I am? You don't *have* kids, do you?"

Fletcher shook his head.

"Then you have no place telling me what my mom might feel. She made me feel like I was insane for years. I have no intention of letting her make me feel that way again."

"I'm sorry, Ryn," Fletcher started to say, but I was already out the door.

" How'd the training session go?" Allie asked when she picked me up.

"Terrible," I said in a clipped tone. "Fletcher was meticulously analyzing every move I made. I'd rather practice with Marek alone."

She wiggled her eyebrows. "What happens when you're alone?"

I scoffed. "Keep dreaming. Nothing happens. Especially lately."

Her expression fell. "What's the deal with you and Marek anyway?"

I bit my lip and looked out the window at the passing houses. "I don't know. After our kiss, he seems… uninterested. It's like the only reason he talks to me is when he's trying to teach me something. Maybe he's waiting for me to make another move. I don't know. Forget about me. What about you and Kyle?"

Allie rolled her eyes. "I don't know how much more obvious I can be with him. He still hasn't asked me out."

"Why don't *you* ask *him* out? I thought you *both* had a thing for each other."

"Yeah, I thought so, too. What if he rejects me?"

I shrugged. "What if?"

"It would ruin the whole dynamic of the group."

I frowned. "Yeah, I guess that's the problem with getting too close to the people you spend so much time with. If it doesn't work out…"

I didn't want to think about that.

Allie pulled up to the cemetery just then. We stepped out of the car silently. I glanced around, wondering where to start. I wasn't sure we'd make it through the whole thing by dark.

"What do you think we're looking for?" I asked.

Allie slipped her keys into her pocket. "I'm not sure. I was hoping you'd know. My guess is that we'll know once we find it." She started down the closest row of headstones.

I followed behind her.

"Hmm…" Allie mused. "These dates don't go back far enough. We should start at some older gravestones."

"I agree," I said, "but I don't know if the cemetery was a good idea in the first place."

"What do you mean?" she asked.

"Maybe a headstone would be too obvious of a marker."

"Depends on how they marked it. They maybe didn't put her name on it. I think we're looking for something more subtle."

"Then how do we know she's not in one of the graves

we've already passed?" I glanced behind me like I might spot her standing there.

"We don't." Allie stopped and turned back to me. "Didn't you say fate brought you to Eagle Valley?"

I shrugged. "I don't know. That's what Fletcher seems to think. Honestly, it's the only thing that makes sense to me."

Allie turned and continued walking. "Right, so if she's here, the Power of Grace should lead you to her, shouldn't it?"

"I want to agree with you, but I feel nothing. I don't know what I'm *supposed* to feel." This trip to the cemetery felt useless. I wanted to go home, but I had to give the place a chance for Allie's sake.

Allie turned down a row of headstones. "I have relatives buried in this row."

I glanced at the dates. "How long has your family been living in Eagle Valley?"

"I think they came in one of the first groups of Davina after the Haylo brothers bought the town. That's just on my dad's side, though. The other side of my family didn't come to America until later. Mom wasn't from Eagle Valley."

I stopped abruptly.

"What?" Allie sounded concerned.

"I just thought of something. If your dad's family was one of the first to settle here, do you think they could've been part of the secret society that protected Grace?"

She drew her eyebrows together like she was thinking

hard. "That would be cool. Now that you mention it, I suppose it's possible."

"Somewhere along the way, they must've stopped handing down the stories about Grace."

Allie nodded. "*I've* never been given any clues that Grace might be here. You think someone else might know where she is? Someone who's still alive?"

I sighed. "I don't know. Even if someone knew, we'd have to figure out who that someone is."

Allie began walking again. "Yeah. It kind of sucks how things are these days. Who knows how many of the stories will be lost over the next few generations?"

"Who knows how much you've already lost?" I asked.

"Here it is." Allie stopped and knelt in front of a grave marker. "This was my great-something-grandma."

I knelt beside her. "It's cool that you're so connected to your family."

"You mean, you don't visit your family's graves often?" she asked curiously.

I shook my head. "I don't even know if some of them are still alive."

I lifted my head and stared into the distance. A tall figure strolled through the other end of the cemetery, but he wasn't close enough to hear us.

"You mean your grandparents?" Allie asked.

My lips turned down at the corners. "I mean my dad."

Allie seemed to realize the mistake she made in prodding for an answer. Her voice softened. "Ryn, I'm sorry."

I shook my head. "No, it's okay. I just think it'd be nice to know where his grave was—if there's one out there for him." I picked at the grass below me. "Mom and I don't know what happened to him. Sometimes… it sounds horrible, but sometimes I *wish* he was dead." I paused. "That came out wrong. I just think it'd be easier knowing that's why he never came back rather than assuming he ran out on us. At the same time, I hope he's out there somewhere and that Mom will find him again."

I lifted my gaze to see that Allie's jaw had gone slack.

"You literally have no idea what happened to your dad?" she asked.

"I literally have no idea." I returned to picking at the grass. "I haven't pressed Mom about it much, either. She doesn't seem to like to talk about him. I think it's too painful for her. Now with all this Davina stuff, I'd like to know more."

"You should talk to your mom about it," Allie suggested.

Ugh. Why were people encouraging me to talk to my mom? She was impossible.

"Maybe knowing more about your dad would help explain things," Allie said. "Like why you have the Power of Grace."

"You think my dad might have something to do with why Grace chose me?"

Allie shrugged. "It's possible. Unless you think your mom's family was Davina, then maybe—"

"There's no way. Mom can't see the demons." My thoughts flew back to one of the most horrifying nights of my life. I'd told Marek about it, but I still hadn't managed to find the right moment to tell Allie.

"Davina powers can skip a generation, you know," Allie pointed out.

I nodded. Marek had told me.

"Even if it skipped my mom, she'd still *know* about the demons. She doesn't. I promise."

Allie seemed to take that as a cue that it was the end of discussion. She got to her feet and glanced around. "Should we try those last few rows and then start weaving our way back?"

I pushed myself to my feet beside her. "Yeah, I think that's best."

I hoped Allie was right and that something would jump out at me, but nothing did. Eventually, we gave up.

"I'm sorry I suggested the cemetery," Allie said on our way back to the car. "I feel like it was a total waste of time."

"Not a *total* waste of time," I said to make her feel better, but it was a lie. "Now we've narrowed the list of places to look."

"Aren't we on a bit of a time limit?" Allie asked. "How long do you think we have now that the Power of Grace has returned?"

I shrugged. That was a question for Fletcher. But Fletcher didn't know I'd had the Power of Grace my whole life—or at least since I was eight and conjured my first purple fireball and killed my first demon. *It's been almost a decade since then. I think the doorway between here and the demon realm can hold out a little longer.*

I tried to convince myself of this, but even the voice in my own head didn't sound believable. I couldn't shake the feeling that I'd been brought to Eagle Valley now because time *was* running out.

"We'll find her," I said with certainty.

I reached for the door handle on the passenger side of Allie's vehicle. Before I could open it, I paused. In the distance, I noticed the same figure I'd seen earlier knelt down next to a nearby headstone.

"What?" Allie followed my gaze.

I didn't take my eyes off him. "Can you give me a couple of minutes?"

Allie opened the driver's side door. "What are you going to say to him?"

I couldn't stop staring at him, as if I could see his grief from fifty yards away. "I'm not sure yet. I think he could use someone to talk to."

I left Allie alone in the car and slowly made my way over to Trenton.

11

"Hey," I said quietly as I approached Trenton. His face lit up when he saw me, but his expression quickly turned to sorrow again.

"Are you okay?" I lowered myself to the grass beside him and gestured to the headstone he'd been staring at. "Someone you know?"

"Not really," he admitted. "Just a distant relative."

I glanced at the words etched into the stone. *Sarah Spencer.*

"You sure?" I asked. "You seem… sad."

Trenton didn't meet my eyes. "I've just heard stories about her. She was my mom's younger sister."

My eyes scanned over Sarah's birth and death dates. She'd died over a decade before Trenton was born. She'd only been a child.

"I'm sorry," I told him honestly. "The stories must be sad."

He nodded somberly.

I didn't know what to say. All I knew was he could use a friend right now.

"What about you?" Trenton lifted his gaze to meet mine. "Do you have any family buried here?"

"No. My family's not from around here."

"Then what are you doing here?" He sounded genuinely curious.

"Oh, um… Allie and I were goofing around."

Trenton blinked a few times. "I saw you earlier. It looked like you two were looking for someone. Did you find her?"

I swallowed. Sure, Trenton didn't seem all that bad, but I wasn't about to tell him about Grace.

"We weren't looking for anyone in particular," I lied. "Just walking."

"Oh," he said flatly. "Because if you were looking for someone, it doesn't hurt to have an extra pair of eyes out there."

"Wouldn't Casey kill you if she thought you were fraternizing with the enemy in any way?" I teased.

A smile twitched at the corner of his lips. "It's possible, but what she doesn't know can't hurt her."

I laughed. "What is it with Casey, anyway?"

Trenton rolled his eyes. "Don't get me started. You don't want to waste your time talking about her."

"Is there a better way to waste my time?" I was glad I was cheering him up.

Trenton looked away from me for a moment. I could just barely see his face flush through the dimming light around us.

"You could waste your time on me," he said.

I was so shocked by his words that my entire body recoiled. Allie had been right. Trenton definitely *was* flirting with me.

"Oh, I…"

"What's the matter?" he asked. "You don't like my company?"

"No. I mean yes. I just…" What was I supposed to say? That I was already in a relationship? One that apparently didn't involve kissing or hand holding or *anything*?

Trenton's smile widened. "It'd be cool to get to know you better."

I couldn't believe what I was hearing. I tucked a strand of brown hair behind my ear and stared down at the grass. "Are you asking me out?"

At least *somebody* was.

"That depends. Do you *want* me to ask you out?"

When I looked back up at him, all traces of sorrow I'd seen earlier had vanished, replaced by a large—and rather sexy—smile.

My thoughts flickered to Marek. This wasn't fair to him, was it?

To hell with Marek, I thought. *If he wanted a relationship, he would've done something about it.*

"We can hang out," I told Trenton.

"Great. Does Friday work for you?"

I couldn't help it when a smile hit my lips. "Yeah, it should."

Trenton stood. "Cool. So, it's a date?"

I rose to my feet beside him. "I guess so."

He stuck his hands in his pockets. "I'll see you later, Ryn."

"Yeah, see you."

I returned to the car with a smile on my face.

"What was that about?" Allie asked once I slid in the passenger seat.

I shrugged and adjusted my seat belt. "I was just trying to cheer him up, and it sort of turned into him asking me out."

"What?" Allie squeaked about two octaves too high. "What about Marek?"

I could feel the heat rise to my face. "I don't know. What *about* Marek? I figured maybe I should keep my options open. Besides, I like Trenton. He's nice." *And hot.*

Allie started the car and shifted into gear. She pursed her lips but remained silent.

"What?" I asked accusingly. Clearly, she had more to say.

She paused for several seconds but finally caved. "I don't get why you're worrying about boys when you should be worrying about Grace."

"I *am* worrying about Grace," I defended harshly.

"You could worry more," Allie mumbled.

"What am I supposed to do? Put my entire life on hold for her? She apparently led me to Eagle Valley. If she's able to communicate with me, maybe she should be more explicit about it."

Allie breathed heavily and stared at the road.

Say something, dammit!

"You're just jealous I have two guys who want my attention and Kyle still hasn't made a move," I snapped.

Allie slammed on the brakes as we reached a stop sign. She turned to me, fuming. "You think I'm *jealous* of you? Do you know what type of friend I am at all? You *should* be putting your life on hold for Grace. Or don't you realize how important it is to find her? She's the only one with power strong enough to keep our world safe."

"If you worship her so much, maybe she should've chosen *you!*" My voice rose. "I didn't ask for any of this. Would you rather have her power? Here! Take it."

A purple fireball formed in my palm. I shoved my hand toward Allie.

She flinched. "Get the hell away from me!"

"Fine." I kicked the door open and swung my backpack over my shoulder as I planted my feet on the pavement.

"Wait, Ryn!" Allie called. "I didn't mean it like that!"

I slammed the door shut and turned my back to her. She remained at the stop sign for several moments. I wasn't sure if she was contemplating getting out of the car to talk to me or if she was waiting for me to come crawling back to her. Before I had a chance to find out, she applied the gas and sped off in front of me.

I was too angry to feel remorse as I watched her go. After a full minute, I finally gave myself a chance to process what just happened.

It was possible I just lost the first real friend I ever had.

I stormed into the house and pounded up the stairs.

"Kathryn," my mom called from the living room.

I paused with one foot on the landing. I took a deep breath before turning back down the steps.

"What?" I didn't intend to sound so hostile.

"Come here," she demanded.

I gritted my teeth and stopped in the doorway to the living room.

Mom looked at me with a pointed expression. "Where have you been? I texted you three times."

"Allie and I were working on our history paper," I lied.

Mom frowned. Clearly, she didn't believe me. "You've been spending an awful lot of time with Allie lately."

"So?" I crossed my arms. "What's wrong with having friends?"

Mom set her crochet hook and yarn aside on the couch.

"There's nothing wrong with having friends. Maybe I just want to spend time with my daughter."

I held back an eye roll. "We never do anything together."

"I still enjoy your company."

She enjoyed when I cooked and cleaned for her.

"Okay," I said. "I'm going to take a shower and go to bed early."

"Hold on," she called before I could make it out of earshot. "What's going on with you lately?"

I turned back to her and sighed heavily. *I'm a Davina and still trying to figure out what it means to be one. All my teachers hate me. My best friend might hate me, too. I've been chosen for a destiny I might not be able to fulfill. The future of the world hinges on me—and I'm not even allowed to entertain the idea of boys to distract myself from that fact.*

"Believe me," I said, "you don't want to know."

"Come here." Mom gestured for me to join her on the couch.

I couldn't come up with a viable excuse to escape. I had no choice but to sit beside her.

Mom placed an arm around my shoulder. I couldn't remember the last time she hugged me. It felt awkward.

"What is it, Kathryn?" she asked like she genuinely cared.

"Nothing," I mumbled with a shrug.

"You can tell me anything," she assured me.

Not anything, I thought. Mom would never know I was a Davina. I'd never tell her I still saw the demons or the fact that I killed one to save her life.

"Kathryn," she repeated sternly.

I stared at her without saying anything.

"Is it about a boy?" she asked.

"What? No!" I drew away from her.

Mom sighed and pulled me closer. "Sometimes I forget you aren't so young anymore. You can come to me with questions."

"About *boys*?" I never pictured my mom and I having *that* conversation.

"I'm not completely clueless," she said. "I *have* dated before. Even before your father."

I wasn't remotely interested in hearing about her sex life.

But there was one thing I *was* interested in hearing about. Was my father a Davina? Did he have something to do with the Power of Grace? Could I pass up an opportunity to learn more about him?

"About my father…" I started.

Mom stiffened beside me. "What about your father?"

"What happened to him?" I asked in a whisper.

Her lips curled down at the corners. "Kathryn, we've talked about this."

"I know, but you never told me the whole story. Isn't there more to it?"

Mom shook her head. "Not really. He walked out on us. That's pretty much the whole story."

"How can we be sure he's not dead or something?"

"I tried looking for him after he left," Mom said, "but I never met his family. I didn't know who to talk to. And now it's been so long…"

"Are there any more specifics?" I pressed. Part of me hoped there was some fantastic story behind his disappearance, like that he'd been a Protector and died a hero.

She sighed. "Why are you asking me this now?"

Because everything has changed.

"Because I've always wanted to know. Now that I'm older, I thought you might actually tell me."

Mom's expression softened. "What is it you want to know?"

"I don't know. Did he say anything before he left?"

She shifted uncomfortably. "You have to understand that your father and I hadn't known each other for long. I thought I was in love with him."

Don't kid yourself, Mom, I wanted to say, *you're still in love with him, even though he left.*

"I'd only just graduated from college," Mom explained. "I moved to a new apartment building. Your father lived across the hall."

I knew all that already, but I didn't want to interrupt her.

"When we met, we instantly clicked. It wasn't long after I met him that I found out I was pregnant." She withdrew her arm from around my shoulder.

I didn't dare move or breathe as the seconds ticked by. I only waited for her to reveal more.

Mom's voice cracked. "I thought it was wonderful news, so I was excited to tell him. He said he was happy, but I could tell he was scared." Her face grew red. "That was the last time I saw him."

"You mean, he left because… because he didn't want me?"

I'd suspected it plenty of times, but I'd never gotten Mom to admit it. Suddenly, my chest felt empty.

"All I know is that he said he had something he had to do, left, and never came back." Mom turned toward the window. "He could've come back whenever he wanted. I waited eight years for it. I guess it took me that long to accept he wasn't coming back."

A lump rose within my throat. Was that it? Was my father a coward who didn't want to face the responsibility of raising me? I'd gotten the impression that Davina were stronger than that.

"What was he afraid of?" My voice rose. "Was he afraid I'd end up like him?"

Her gaze flew to mine. "End up like him how?"

I gritted my teeth. "He never mentioned anything to you? You never thought he might be… different?"

Mom tilted her head in question. "You think he might've had mental issues?"

I could hear the last bit she'd left out. *Mental issues like you.* She thought I was talking about my insanity—the craziness that never existed in the first place.

"Never mind," I said quietly. I quickly diverted the conversation. "So, you stopped waiting for him. What have you been doing since, Mom?"

She blinked. "What do you mean?"

I'd never voiced my thoughts aloud to her. "We've moved every year since I was eight. Have you been running away from something or running toward something?"

Mom opened her mouth but quickly shut it. It was like she couldn't believe I'd ask such a question. The way her eyes widened told me she wasn't sure of the answer.

I rose from the couch.

"No, Kathryn," she insisted in a harsh tone. "You don't just get to leave in the middle of an uncomfortable conversation."

I turned back to her. "I'm not, Mom. The conversation is over."

I hurried out of the room and up the stairs. In my bedroom, I fell to my bed. My gaze landed on the map still tacked to the wall across the room. My eyes scanned the image as though something might actually pop out at me this time. One thing became clear the longer I stared. If my father never cared about me, he sure as hell didn't deserve my attention.

Right now, I had to focus on Grace and getting my best friend back.

13

No matter how many times I rehearsed my apology speech in my head Thursday morning, I never pictured having to chase Allie down. I expected to apologize to her on the way to school, but she didn't offer to drive me.

I ended up power walking to class and arrived just as the warning bell rang. I didn't have time to find Allie to tell her I was sorry for the way I acted. I waited for her at our lockers between first and second period, but she avoided my gaze and stepped into Fletcher's classroom without a word.

"Allie," I called from behind her.

She slid into a chair in the corner of the room like she hadn't heard me. Kyle took the seat next to her so I couldn't sit by her like usual.

Allie even avoided me during lunch. She and Kyle left the lunchroom with their trays—probably to sit around the fireplace in the common room. Marek had to talk me out of chasing after her. He told me to give her some space and that she'd cool off eventually.

Between Allie giving me the cold shoulder and the mounting stress of searching for Grace, I found it hard to focus on anything. After school in Fletcher's classroom, my essence flickered like a strobe light between white and purple.

"Whoa." Marek backed away like he was scared my magic might explode.

"Something on your mind?" Fletcher asked. I knew he'd been watching me from behind his desk.

I turned to him and crossed my arms. "Actually, yes. Why am *I* the only one who has to search for Grace?"

Fletcher blinked several times. "You're the one connected to her."

"Can't you help, I don't know… look for *clues*?" I threw my arms out in frustration and fell into one of the desks nearby.

"I am," Fletcher assured me, gesturing to the books spread out in front of him.

"Okay, but I mean actively. Elizabeth said the school is one of the oldest buildings in town. Shouldn't we search the building or something?"

"You think she might be here, at Galen?" Fletcher asked in thought.

"Why not?" I said. "This property has been protected by Davina for decades. Whether that was by design or because the rest of you are connected to her somehow, I don't know. I just think it's worth taking a look."

Fletcher pondered the theory for several moments. "Where do you suggest we start?"

I glanced to Marek like he might have an answer. He leaned against one of the desks, deep in thought.

I turned back to Fletcher. He looked at me like I was supposed to magically know the answer, but I was afraid I'd only disappoint him. I wasn't exactly running on instinct here.

I shrugged. "We might as well start on one side of the building and work our way to the other."

"Okay." Fletcher stood.

I quickly realized I had no idea what I was doing. I let Fletcher take the lead, and we strolled slowly from classroom to classroom. Every so often, Marek asked if I knew what I was looking for or if I felt anything.

"No," I told him.

Of course I felt *something*, but it wasn't related to Grace. It was that damn boy next to me sending my heart haywire. When I looked at him, I felt as equally irritated with him as I was attracted to him. Maybe Trenton *was* the better choice. He didn't make me feel so irrational.

By the time we covered the entire first and second floors of the building, I still wasn't ready to give up. That would mean less time with Marek. As much as I hated how confused he made me, I wanted to spend as much time with him as I could.

"Does the school have a basement?" I asked Fletcher.

"Yes," he said. "Good thinking."

Fletcher led us to a door that opened to a dark flight of stairs. When we reached the bottom, it wasn't anything like

I expected. I thought we'd find a maze of hallways and storage rooms. Instead, it was simply one vast, empty room interrupted only by support pillars. A musty scent filled the cool air, and the stone foundation looked ancient. The entire space was covered in a thick layer of dust.

"There's not much down here," Fletcher said. "Mostly only maintenance comes down for the furnace."

I pulled my phone out of my back pocket and turned on the flashlight. The small light was almost enough to bathe the large room.

"Hold on." Fletcher returned to the top of the stairs. A moment later, light flooded the basement from overhead bulbs. "That should help." He pounded down the stairs and stopped beside Marek and me.

I glanced around, looking for anything that might draw my attention. "Does it go any further back?"

"No," Fletcher answered.

I began my way around the perimeter of the room.

"You said no one ever comes down here?" Marek asked Fletcher.

"No, not really."

"It seems like so much wasted space," Marek pointed out.

"It can get wet in the spring," Fletcher explained, "so it's not exactly ideal for storage. Finding anything, Ryn?"

"No," I said in disappointment.

"If no one uses the space, maybe we could train down here," Marek suggested.

"That's not a bad idea," Fletcher agreed. "There's enough room, and you don't run the risk of anyone seeing you. I *may* be able to snag an old target from storage that you can start on."

I whirled around. "Really? You're going to let me start using my essence? Like, doing more than just conjuring it?"

Fletcher nodded. "I think you're ready for it."

I smiled. "This is great!"

Fletcher glanced at his watch. "Maybe we should call it a day. I'm sorry we didn't find anything."

He sounded genuinely discouraged, like he might be having doubts about Grace being in Eagle Valley at all. I couldn't say I hadn't wondered the same thing myself.

When we returned to Fletcher's classroom, I gathered up my bag and headed out of the building.

"Hey, Ryn," Marek called, catching up to me.

My heart soared at the sound of his voice. "Yeah?"

"What do you say we head down to the valley?" He wiggled his eyebrows at me. His smile was so sexy; I'd agree to anything he suggested.

Somehow, I managed to keep my cool. "I thought you didn't want to train there anymore."

"It's not for training. It's for fun." His smile widened.

"What kind of fun?"

If he was talking about making out, I was all for it.

Marek nudged me with his elbow like I was being silly. "Flying, of course."

Well, it wasn't making out, but I was still eager to join him.

"Do we get to race?" I asked hopefully.

"Of course we'll race," he said.

"Ready?"

"Huh?" He shot me a questioning expression.

"Set, go!"

I took off running toward the back of the school, but it didn't take long for his footsteps to catch up and his long legs to push forward in front of me. Marek pulled his shirt off his head as he sprinted down the trail to the valley. I just barely caught a glimpse of the scars on his back.

He tossed his shirt aside when we reached the clearing. Without slowing, I dropped my bag to the ground, stripped off my cardigan, and leapt into the air.

For the first time in days, I felt like I wasn't just some girl Marek was forced to teach. We were actually friends.

I hope we end up being more, I found myself thinking.

And then I remembered I had a date with Trenton the following evening. Why was my heart being pulled in two different directions?

14

"*Did* you find who you were looking for?" Trenton asked when I met up with him at Angela's Café on Friday evening.

"What?" I asked breathlessly.

I'd lost track of the time after school during my training session with Marek. It was thrilling to finally be able to aim my magic at something—and I'd come to find I wasn't a bad shot. I guess being in softball in junior high had paid off. I'd rushed home afterwards to shower. I never told Marek where I was headed.

Trenton's eyes followed me as I lowered myself into the seat across from him. "You said you were looking for someone in the cemetery."

"Did I? No. Allie was just taking me to see her family's graves."

Trenton nodded. "How was the first week of school? Up to anything fun?"

I flipped my menu open. "I wouldn't call homework fun. The training is usually fun, though."

"You're training outside of school?" he asked.

I suddenly realized I'd said too much. "Doesn't everyone? I see you with Casey and Troy in the valley all the time."

"Yeah, but I haven't seen you around."

"I don't like training in the valley," I lied. "I haven't had as much training as the rest of you, so I'd rather not embarrass myself in front of an audience."

Trenton nodded. "Where do you find the time to train between all the other running around you do?"

I glanced up from my menu. "What do you mean?"

"The park, the library, the cemetery... I always see you hanging somewhere around town."

"Are you stalking me?" I accused lightheartedly.

Trenton set down his menu and leaned his elbows on the table. He spoke in a whisper. "So what if I am?"

If he was going for sexy with the way he stared at me, it definitely worked. Something in his eyes hinted at danger, but in a way I wanted to be a part of. It took me off guard, considering Trenton was more like the jocks at my old schools than anything. *Marek* was the one who screamed danger, with his leather jacket, motorcycle, and knack for saving my life.

So why did it feel like I could enjoy the danger in Trenton's eyes just as well?

"Well, it's a little creepy, but flattering." I turned back to the menu and let my brown hair fall in front of me. Hopefully it helped conceal the blush rising to my cheeks.

"At least I have the flattering part down," Trenton teased with a smile. "You know what you want to order?"

I closed my menu. "Yeah, I think I do."

I didn't mind hanging out with Trenton, but every so often, I found my mind wandering back to Marek. What was he up to right now? Did he ever think about me while we were apart?

Trenton was nice. He even offered to pay for my food. By the end of dinner, I thought I might agree to a second date if he asked.

I was smiling when we walked out of the café together, but that smile quickly vanished. Dread filled me the moment I spotted blond hair swaying in the wind. I froze in front of Celeste's, the cute jewelry store I hadn't had a chance to check out yet.

"Trenton!" Casey called from a few shops away. She hurried past a group of five teens I didn't know.

Troy followed behind her.

"Where have you been? Troy and I have been looking —" Her eyes caught mine, and a hard expression settled on her face. She stopped in front of us and crossed her arms. "Really, Trenton?"

He glanced at me and shrugged like he didn't know what she was talking about.

"You ditched us to hang out with *her*?"

Trenton didn't seem at all fazed by Casey's attitude. "I told you I had plans tonight."

"Oh, Trenton," she said like he was a child. "I didn't think you meant with one of *them*."

"What's your problem with my group?" I snapped. It seemed like she was only mean for the sake of being mean.

She raised her blond brows. "Maybe you should ask your *group*. They're the ones who had a problem with *me* first. I'm only returning the favor."

"Come on," Trenton said with a sigh. "Give Ryn a break."

I appreciated that he was sticking up for me.

Casey looked to Troy like she couldn't believe what she was hearing and wanted him to help her out. Her gaze quickly returned to Trenton. "If you're going to ditch us, Trenton, you should at least date someone who can conjure essence."

"Shh…" Trenton hissed and glanced toward the group of people nearby.

I barely heard him over my own outburst. "Who says I can't?"

Casey scoffed. "Puh-lease. We've run into your team enough times, and I've never seen you conjure essence. All you can do is fly. Based on what I've seen, you're not very good at that, either. What was it Allie said the first time we met? You have amazing powers or something? I'd like to see that one day."

I couldn't stop myself as irritation bubbled to the surface. My brows constricted, and my breaths grew shallow. A wave of heat passed over my skin as anger consumed me. It was like I was watching myself from above, unable to control my own body.

"You wanna see?" I challenged.

I drew my arm back. Inside my palm, a white orb

glowed in warning. I aimed for her face. Before I could throw the essence, Trenton's hand caught my wrist.

"She's not worth it," he said.

"Whoa." Casey took a step back and held her hands up. She didn't sound the least bit surprised, only amused.

I closed my fist as my anger subsided. Trenton loosened his grip, and I dropped my empty hand to my side. Shit. I shouldn't have done that. I took several steps back.

The group beyond Casey shot glances our way and whispered amongst themselves. There was no question that they'd seen my outburst.

Casey smiled like she was entertained. "You might be new here, but you should know conjuring essence in public places is off limits."

I swallowed the lump in my throat.

"Come on, Casey," Trenton pleaded. "Don't tell on her."

Casey narrowed her eyes at Trenton. Apparently, she wasn't used to being told what to do.

"You remember how I was when I came here," Trenton said.

Casey paused and then slowly nodded. "Oh, now I see. You like the new girl because you have something in common. How sweet."

I wanted to conjure another fireball and throw it at her head. I couldn't stand the condescension in her tone. Somehow, I managed to keep my fists clenched at my side. I literally bit down on my tongue to keep the nasty words I had for her from spilling out of my mouth.

"Fine, Trenton," she said, turning on her heel. "Have fun. Just be ready for our battle next week, okay?"

Trenton and I remained frozen on the sidewalk as she and Troy distanced themselves from us. I noticed the group nearby staring.

"What?" I snapped. "Never seen a phone before?"

I reached into my pocket and flashed my phone's screen at them. Because they'd *totally* believe that's what was glowing in my hand.

One guy scoffed, and the group turned away from us.

Trenton placed a cool hand on my arm.

I forced myself to lift my gaze. "I'm a freaking idiot. I should have—I can't believe… Thank you for sticking up for me."

He smiled. "What are friends for?" He draped his arm around my shoulder. "Maybe we should get you home."

I nodded. "Thank you."

Trenton led me over to his vehicle and opened the passenger side door for me. My hands shook. That wasn't the first time I'd let humans see my essence. What if people at Eagle Valley High started talking about me and connected the two incidents? Instead of saving the Davina like I was chosen to, I was going to lead them to their destruction by revealing their secret.

Great choice, Grace.

"I'm sorry," I said as Trenton drove down the street. "I just get so caught up in the fight sometimes."

"It's fine, Ryn," he assured me. "It happens. Just don't mention it to anyone, okay? You could get in serious trouble."

"I won't," I promised.

Trenton kept his eyes on the road. "Where do I turn?"

I gave Trenton directions back to my house, and we arrived within minutes.

"Are you up to anything this weekend?" he asked when I stepped out of the car. "We could hang out."

Before I could answer, a second car approached. I looked up to see Allie stepping out of Kyle's red compact car. She stopped in her tracks the moment she saw me. Allie's voice warning me not to get too distracted with boys entered my mind.

"Trenton, I'm sorry. I'm busy."

"Doing what?"

Training. Searching for an ancient Davina. Probably failing at both.

"Homework," I lied. *And I need to talk to Allie.*

"That can't take you *all* weekend."

Allie began walking toward her house. My eyes followed her.

"Sorry, Trenton. I have to go. I'll see you on Monday at school." I closed the door and turned toward Allie. I barely registered the sound of Trenton's car pulling away from the curb as I tried to work up the courage to call out to my best friend.

"Allie!" I heard her name escape my lips.

A strange silence settled over the night as we stared at each other across our lawns.

I took a deep breath. My apology had to come now or never.

15

"Allie," I called as I crossed my lawn onto hers. "We need to talk."

Her jaw tensed, but she didn't object. She crossed her arms, waiting for me to say more.

The whole speech I'd prepared earlier completely fell from my mind the moment I faced her.

"Well?" she prodded.

Silence hung over the lawn as I struggled to find the right words.

"I'm sorry," I managed in a small voice. "I acted like a self-obsessed idiot."

Allie smirked. "At least you admit it."

"I don't want to keep fighting," I told her.

"You could've apologized sooner," she said in a bitter tone.

"I tried!" I defended. "You've been avoiding me for two days."

Allie stared at me without saying anything. I searched

her eyes for signs of what she was thinking, but I couldn't read her.

"I still want your help finding Grace," I said.

Allie pursed her lips. "Are you sure? You're not afraid I'll get jealous?"

I sighed heavily. "I didn't mean it about the jealousy thing. I'm just overwhelmed. I'm sorry I took it out on you."

Her gaze dropped to the grass.

After several moments of silence, I spoke again. "I miss you, Allie. I can't do this without you."

A smile crossed her face when she looked up at me. "That's all I wanted to hear. Okay, I'll help you."

That was it? No yelling? No blame? I suddenly realized how lucky I was to call Allie my friend.

"Thank you," I said.

"So, we'll check out the library again in the morning?" she asked eagerly.

Dread filled me. I wasn't looking forward to another failed mission.

"That's it!" I threw my hands up the following day. "I'm completely out of ideas."

Just as I suspected, our search through the library on Saturday morning had been useless. I thought for sure we'd been missing something. I even turned to pulling at books on the shelves to see if they'd open any secret passageways. As cool as that would be, nothing happened.

If I was this close to Grace, I figured I'd feel a pull toward her. The likelihood of her not being in Eagle Valley at all was growing more and more plausible by the day.

I suggested we return to my house around noon. Though Allie was disappointed that our last lead hadn't turned up any clues, she agreed with me.

"I don't get it," she complained as she plopped down on my bed. "Fletcher's theory made so much sense. What else would've brought you to Eagle Valley if Grace wasn't here?"

"I know." I slumped onto the bed beside her. "I've been going through the same thing over and over in my head, too. Maybe…" I bit my lip in thought.

"What?" she asked curiously.

I sighed and stood to pace around the room. "Maybe she's not here at all. What if Fletcher got part of the story wrong?"

"Which part?"

I couldn't believe I was suggesting it. "What if we're not looking for a grave or a body? What if Grace isn't a real person?"

Allie drew her eyebrows together, looking more confused than ever. "What are you suggesting?"

I raised my palm. Inside it grew a purple orb. "What if the Power of Grace *is* Grace? What if they're the same thing?"

She eyed me skeptically. "Are you saying you think you could close the portal to the demon realm on your own?"

Theories and doubts raced through my mind. "I don't know. How do we even know the realm is opening?"

Allie looked at me like I was crazy. "Because the power of the Originals is supposed to return when the world is in danger. Just the fact that you're here, with the Power of Grace, is a *sign*, Ryn."

I stopped pacing abruptly. "What if the stories are wrong?"

"I don't think so, Ryn. I've been hearing these stories my whole life. I mean, I never thought I'd live to see the day, but…"

I fell into the chair next to my desk. "You heard what Elizabeth said. A lot of these stories are passed down orally. The truth could've easily been lost from one generation to the next."

The skepticism deepened on Allie's face. "Just because we haven't found Grace yet doesn't mean the stories aren't true."

"It's not just that," I said.

"What do you mean?" She sounded annoyed.

I took a deep breath. I didn't know if I was ready to tell Allie, but I had to give her some sort of answer. "Because, Allie, I've had the Power of Grace for a long time."

"Wait." Allie shot to her feet. "You knew you had the Power of Grace before you came to Eagle Valley?"

"No! Of course not! I didn't know *what* it was."

Allie's eyes widened. "We don't know how much time we have, but this means we have even less time!"

I calmed my voice. "Sit down, Allie. I think there's something you should know."

She followed my command but never took her eyes off me.

"I was eight the first time I used the Power of Grace," I admitted.

I told Allie about Clinton, the demon who befriended me when I was a child. I told her how he had fed on my mom's essence and convinced her to attempt suicide. I told her how I'd walked in on it, how I saw a purple ball of energy erupt from my palm, and how Clinton had disappeared before my eyes. I told her how I wrapped my mother's wrists in the bed sheet and saved her life.

A lump rose to my throat as I finished the story.

Allie stood from the bed and slowly walked over to me. She wrapped me into a hug before speaking. "Ryn, I am *so* sorry."

"It's okay." My voice cracked. "It happened a long time ago."

Allie squeezed me one more time. "What do you think it means? Do you think after all this time the demon realm could've opened by now?"

"I don't know." I shrugged. "Wouldn't that mean the end of the world? I mean, the demons would flood into this realm, kill us, and feed off human essence. There'd be too many of them."

"Maybe there aren't any demons left in their realm," Allie theorized. "They closed the portals so long ago; they could've died off. We'd have no way of knowing."

I rubbed my hands over my face. "There's so much to speculate about. It's a lot to take in."

Allie raised her brows. "Tell me about it. I've grown up with these stories, and to think that they might not be accurate... It's like abandoning my whole belief system."

She paused for a moment. "Maybe there's another explanation."

"Like what?"

Allie's hands rested on the back of my chair. "Well, you've gone nearly a decade without using the Power of Grace, haven't you? It was just the one time when you were a kid and then here in Eagle Valley?"

I looked up at her and nodded.

"Maybe the portals *were* a threat when you were a kid, but something happened and they weren't anymore. And now the risk is there again."

"You think the Power of Grace left me and then came back?"

Allie dropped her gaze. "I don't know. It's just another theory to add to the ever-growing pile."

"It's not a bad one. I just wish someone actually knew the truth. I sure as hell don't feel like I know what's going on here."

Allie laughed lightly. "I'm sure if we found Grace, she could tell us."

I raised my brows. "You still think we have a chance?"

"I think there *has* to be truth to these stories," she said as she returned to sit on the bed. "Even the demons know about them. I think we've missed something important."

I sighed. "So, what? We're back to square one?"

"We *could* try checking out the library and the school again. There are lots of places to look in those buildings. Or maybe we can try a new place, like somewhere that existed during the early settlement but got torn down or something."

I rubbed my fingers across my eyes. "I don't know, Allie." *I don't know what to believe anymore.*

She already had her phone out. "Let's go back through some of those articles we found. Maybe we missed something."

I didn't know what else we could possibly do. It was either follow Allie's suggestion or give up completely and admit the stories meant nothing, that I was just some anomaly rather than the chosen one.

"Kathryn," my mother's voice called from down the hall.

I stood and hurried to my door. "What?"

"You have company."

"Okay, I'll be there in a minute," I shouted back.

Allie placed her phone back in her pocket. "Expecting someone?"

"Not at all." I crossed the room and glanced out the window that looked over the front lawn. Kyle's car was parked near the curb.

Allie peeked out the window beside me. "I hope *he* has good news."

I turned to her. "Let's go find out."

16

We descended the stairs to find Marek and Kyle standing in my front hallway. My heart flipped at the sight of Marek. He looked sexier than ever with disheveled hair and his leather jacket on. His hands were shoved in his jean pockets.

Mom returned to the living room to work on crocheting a third scarf.

"What's up?" I asked.

Marek shrugged. "Not much. We were bored and wanted to see if you guys wanted to…" He glanced toward the living room to check that my mom wouldn't overhear. "Work out?"

I sucked in a breath. "Actually, we were kind of working on something."

"Oh." Disappointment entered his tone.

"You're free to join us," I offered immediately.

He perked up. "Great. What are you working on?"

Allie dropped her voice to a low whisper. "What else? Looking for Grace."

"Should we go back up to my room?" I suggested.

The four of us made it halfway up the stairs before Mom's eye caught mine from the living room.

"You know the rules, Kathryn," she called. "You can hang out in the kitchen."

I sighed heavily. I thought she'd trust me with boys by now. When I turned around and caught a whiff of Marek's scent, I realized even *I* didn't trust myself around boys… at least, not this one.

We headed down the hall and into the kitchen.

Marek's chair screeched across the hardwood floor as he scooted himself closer to the table. "Fill us in on what you've been working on."

"Not much," I admitted in disappointment.

"Mostly coming up with dumb theories," Allie told him.

"They're not *all* dumb," I defended.

Kyle raised a curious eyebrow. "What kind of theories?"

We quickly filled them in on our conversation from earlier, making sure to keep our voices low so my mom wouldn't hear.

"I agree with Ryn," Marek said. "They're not *all* dumb."

I smiled proudly, but that smile quickly faded.

"But I also agree with Allie," he said. "These stories about the power of the Originals returning when the human realm is threatened are too prevalent to dismiss."

"Couldn't they just be old legends?" I argued.

"They're not just *stories*." Kyle sounded offended.

"Yeah," Allie agreed.

I held up my hands in surrender. "Okay. You don't have to gang up on me."

"We weren't," Kyle said.

I shot him a hard glance. "Anyway, Allie and I were going to review some of the news articles we took pictures of when we were at the library. We could've missed something. Unless you had any other theories."

I could tell by the look on the guys' faces that they were just as clueless as we were.

Allie and I pulled out our phones again. Kyle scooted his chair closer to Allie.

Marek rounded the table to stand behind me and look at my screen. He rested one arm on the back of my chair and the other on the table next to me. We nearly touched. It definitely didn't help my concentration. Even the rhythm of his breathing sent my heart summersaulting inside my chest.

Eventually, Marek grew tired of standing and pulled a chair over beside me. Our knees touched under the table. I couldn't tell if it was intentional or not. Either way, the surface of my skin heated a few degrees. I wasn't quite sure how he didn't notice my heart trying to beat its way out of my chest at his touch. I had to set my phone down between us to hide my trembling fingers.

How am I supposed to function when he insists on distracting me like this?

Marek looked between Allie and Kyle as soon as we finished scanning our final article. "You find anything useful?"

"No," she said in disappointment.

"Maybe we should go back to the library," I suggested. "There could be more news articles we never got a chance to read."

"What do you think we'll find in them if we haven't found anything here?" Allie asked.

She placed her phone into Marek's outstretched hand. He began scrolling through the pictures.

"I don't know," I admitted. "A mention of an old building. Maybe even a mention of Grace."

"I don't think anyone would've risked mentioning her in the paper," Marek said without taking his eyes off the screen.

I knew he was right. I rested my face in my hand and stared at the screen with him. He used two fingers to zoom out of the picture he'd been looking at and then scrolled on to the next one.

My hand shot out and grabbed his wrist. "Hold on. Go back to that last one."

My breath completely left my chest. I grabbed the phone out of his hands to examine the picture closer.

"Why didn't you mention this?" I demanded, turning the screen toward Allie.

"Mention what?" she asked innocently.

"This picture on that page! Don't you recognize that house?"

Allie squinted at the screen. "No."

"Look closer." I shoved the screen toward her.

She eyed the article and drew in a sharp breath. "Oh my gosh! I didn't realize. It looks so different. There are more trees, and the porch is missing. They must've added it on later..."

I looked back at the screen and zoomed in on the article. "Built in 1858, it says. I knew the house was old, but I never would've guessed it was *that* old."

Kyle slowly reached out to take the phone from me. He examined the image. "So it's a picture of your house. What does it mean?"

I gazed at him wide-eyed. Didn't he understand it meant someone from Praesid built this house and lived here?

"It means we found her!" I was unable to contain my excitement. "Guys, we found Grace!"

17

I leapt out of my chair. "Allie, you were right!"

"About what?"

"Everything!" I exclaimed. "About fate bringing me here. You kept saying I should've sensed Grace, and I did. Every time we went looking for her, I wanted to go home. I thought I was just feeling discouraged, but it wasn't that. It's because she's here, in my house!"

I rushed out of the kitchen and took the stairs down to the basement two at a time. Three pairs of footsteps followed behind me.

"Allie, remember when we tried out the dart thing?" I didn't wait for an answer. "The dart landed in the floor at first because it was *literally* showing me where Grace was. Here, take this."

I shoved a paint can into Marek's hands and bent to inspect the carving of the Davina woman I'd found two weeks ago.

"This has to be it," I said.

108

Allie and Marek both inched closer to view the carving etched into the stone foundation.

"This *means* something," I insisted. "It was only after I found this that I spread my wings for the first time. It's because it *spoke* to me. It *inspired* me. Help me move this stuff."

The three of them went speechless. They stared at me for a moment as I began pulling things off the shelf.

"Come on," I insisted, unable to contain my excitement.

Marek set the paint can aside and began removing random household items our landlord had left for storage. Allie and Kyle quickly joined in.

"That should be good," I said before situating myself on one end of the shelf.

Marek gripped onto the other side. Together, we slid the shelf across the floor. It screeched along the concrete.

I quickly dropped to my knees to get closer to the carving. A shiver ran down my spine as I grazed my fingers across it. "She's here. I know it."

"How do you know?" Allie asked curiously.

"I just do." I took a deep breath and stood, retreating several steps to get a better look. "There has to be a door or something."

I returned to the wall and ran my hand over the worn stones in search of a seam of some sort. I found nothing.

"She's right behind this wall," I said, more to myself than anyone else.

I closed my eyes and focused on my body. A sensation I'd never noticed before coursed through my veins, like my magic was drawing me toward Grace.

When my eyes opened, a purple glow emanated from my fingertips. I completely forgot my friends were standing beside me as I reached out and placed my glowing hands to the wall.

I held my breath, waiting.

Nothing happened.

"Come on," I said through gritted teeth. I pushed my palms harder against the stone.

I don't know how long I stood there. Eventually, I heard someone shift behind me, reminding me that I wasn't alone. I dropped my hands and turned to my friends. They stared at me with wide eyes.

"How do we get to her?" I asked, as if one of them might know the answer.

"Maybe it's not a door," Kyle theorized. "Maybe it's a clue."

"I don't know…" Marek stepped forward to give the wall his own inspection.

"Hold on." I stuck my arm out and caught him by the shoulder.

Confusion settled on his face, but he stepped out of the way.

"Maybe this'll work." I took a deep breath and opened my palm, concentrating on the magic pulsing through my body. A bright purple orb hovered millimeters above my skin. Pulling my arm back, I heaved the essence toward the carving. It exploded against the wall but did nothing more than wiggle the shelf we'd just moved.

I turned away in frustration. Marek stepped forward

again. Beside him, Kyle ran his hands along the stone wall. Allie remained frozen in place.

I glanced around the room like it might hold answers. My eyes fell upon the pile of junk we'd removed from the shelf. I bent to riffle through it until my fingers closed around a cool wooden handle.

"Stand back," I warned.

Marek jumped out of the way just in time for me to swing a hammer at the stone in front of me. It didn't so much as chip away the wall. I pulled my arm back to take another shot at it, but Marek caught my wrist.

"Slow down, Ryn," he ordered.

I was so caught up in finding a way through the wall that I didn't have time to think about the fact that Marek was touching me.

My eyes locked on his, but I felt more annoyed that he'd stopped me than anything. "We have to get through somehow."

"And we will," he promised.

I dropped the hand holding the hammer to my side to show him I was listening, but I couldn't manage to slow my quick, shallow breaths.

"Look." Marek pointed to a small cavity in the stone just below the outline of the Davina woman.

Allie and I both drew closer to inspect it.

I, personally, saw nothing significant about it.

"And?" I asked, looking up at him.

He raised his eyebrows like he couldn't believe I didn't get it. "Look closer."

I did, even going so far as to stick my finger in the hole and feel around. My fingernail caught on a small crack running vertically along the inside of it. I bent to look inside. Realization and disappointment struck me simultaneously.

"A keyhole," I said. It wasn't a question.

Marek nodded.

Kyle knelt next to the hole to take a look.

I paced around the room. "Great. So now that we've found her, we have to find a *key*, too. That could be anywhere!"

I rushed back over to the wall and stuck my finger inside the hole, channeling my magic toward it.

Marek stopped me by taking ahold of my wrist before I could get too far. "Be careful. You don't want to damage the lock, do you?"

"How do you know this won't get us through?" I raised a challenging eyebrow.

"Maybe Kyle was right. Maybe it's not a door. Maybe she's not right here." Marek patted the wall.

"We can at least find out!" I cried.

"That's not what I meant." Marek ran his fingers through his hair like he always did when he became frustrated. I couldn't help but think he was frustrated with *me*. "I meant that maybe the door is somewhere else and this is just the spot that unlocks it."

Marek began pacing along the basement wall like he was looking for a secret passageway. Kyle started on the other side of the room to help look.

"Where?" I asked rhetorically. "I don't see a door, Marek. She's *here*, right behind this carving. I can *feel* it."

Marek tore his gaze from the wall. "Okay, but I still don't think we should destroy the lock."

"What does it matter as long as we get through?" I argued. "I don't see any keys lying around nearby, do you?"

He continued around the room without answering.

I turned back to Allie, hoping she'd agree with me.

It took her a moment to catch me staring. "What? Don't ask me. I don't have any ideas."

"Maybe we should call Fletcher," Kyle suggested from across the room.

My shoulders relaxed slightly. "Fine."

Allie already had her phone out. She snapped a picture of the carving on the wall. While she contacted Fletcher and caught him up on what was happening, I sat on the cold basement floor and stared at the wall in front of me. I still couldn't process the reality of the situation.

"Grace," I mumbled under my breath, "how can you be so close yet so far out of reach?"

I managed to get my mom out of the house by convincing her I needed a fluffy purple scarf. I knew she didn't have the yarn for it and would have to make a trip to the craft store. She seemed positively pleased that I was taking an interest in her hobby.

She should've known me better than that.

Marek and Kyle made a show of getting into Kyle's car to leave. Mom wouldn't have let them stay when she wasn't around.

Fletcher showed up a few minutes later. He stood in front of the wall the whole time with his chin rested on his fist and his brow furrowed in deep thought.

"I'll have to go through my history books again," he said.

I knew that meant he didn't have any ideas.

Fletcher, Marek, and Kyle left a few minutes before my mom arrived home. Shortly after, Allie headed home, too.

I returned to the basement and didn't take my eyes off the Davina carving as I lowered myself to the cold floor and crossed my legs. A soothing stillness settled over the basement. Closing my eyes, I tensed my shoulder and felt the familiar sensation of my wings sprouting out of my back. I thought it might help me relax and get in tune with Grace.

I become so consumed in thoughts of how to get through to her that I didn't hear my mother calling for me from upstairs. I didn't hear the door to the basement open or her footsteps descend the steps.

But I heard her audible intake of breath when she saw me sitting there, white wings sprouted from my back and everything.

18

Isprang to my feet and whirled around to face her. I forgot to account for the extra space I took up, and my wings scraped painfully along the stone wall.

"Mom!"

"Kathryn!" She froze.

I pulled my wings into me, but it was too late. Mom's knees shook, and she sank down onto a step in the middle of the staircase. One hand tightened around the railing.

I crossed the basement and climbed the stairs to sit next to her. "Mom, it's okay."

I reached out to place my hand on hers, but she recoiled and stared at me in shock. Her mouth opened, but no sound came out.

"Calm down, Mom," I insisted. "I can explain everything."

Mom finally blinked and dropped her hand from the

railing. She brushed her bangs from her eyes, but her gaze never met mine.

"Sorry," she said in a dazed voice. "I don't know what came over me. I just got lightheaded. I think I'm going to go lie down."

Mom rose and started up the stairs.

I shot to my feet. "That's it?"

What the hell?

She stopped at the basement door and finally looked at me. "What?"

"We're not even going to *talk* about this?" I demanded.

The time had come to tell her the truth, and she was just going to walk away from it? I could be cruel; I could let her believe she was going insane like she'd done to me my whole life. But this was my chance to finally convince her I wasn't crazy. After all this time, I needed to hear her admit she was wrong.

"I'm just lightheaded is all," she insisted.

"No," I said in a strong voice. "You *saw* my wings."

"What are you talking about?" Her voice shook. I could hear it in her tone; she feared we were sharing in the same delusion.

"I'm not crazy," I said. "And neither are you."

My frustrations grew the longer she stared at me without speaking.

I gritted my teeth and pushed past her into the hallway. "I'll show you!"

I stopped in the living room and tensed my shoulders. White feathery wings sprouted from my back. Mom's eyes widened from where she stood in the doorway. She took a step back and steadied herself against the wall.

"Ever heard of the Davina, Mom?"

"The what?" she asked like she hadn't heard me.

"The Davina," I repeated. "They're like angels. I'm one of them."

Mom shook her head like she couldn't believe what she was hearing. "This isn't happening," she mumbled to herself.

I gritted my teeth. This was happening whether she liked it or not. She was *not* going to make me feel ashamed about it. I had half a mind to slap her across the face and snap her out of her shocked daze.

"Pull yourself together, Mom," I said in a strict voice.

"Don't you use that tone with me," she replied instinctively.

There's the mom I know.

I took a deep breath. "Can you please sit down so we can talk about this?"

She hesitated.

"Please," I begged.

Mom inched along the perimeter of the room like she was trying to keep her distance from me. She sat on the couch and never took her eyes off my wings.

I sank into the loveseat across from her. "Let me explain."

From there, the confessions tumbled out of me. I repeated the stories of the Davina and the demons Fletcher had told me. I told her about Grace and how I had access to her powers. I admitted Grace was in our basement and that it was my destiny to awaken her.

Mom remained silent the whole time I spoke. I had no clue what she was thinking until I finally finished my story.

"Kathryn, this is insane," she said, as if trying to convince us both of that. "Even if it were true, do you really think I'd let you go fight on the front lines of some ancient war?"

She might as well have punched me in the gut the way her words hit me.

"You don't have a choice," I snapped.

"As long as I'm your mother, I do," she argued. "You're not an adult yet."

"What does that matter? This is something I really want to do, Mom."

"You do?" she asked in surprise.

Did I mean it? I contemplated the question for several moments. I wasn't interested in killing demons, but I still wanted to help the Davina. I still wanted to wake Grace.

"Yeah, I do," I said. "It's the first time I've really felt like I was meant for something."

I literally *was* meant to awaken Grace, but it was more than that. There was a passion that came with it that I'd never felt before.

Mom shook her head sternly. "If what you're saying is true, you could be in serious danger."

And I hadn't even told her about Dorian yet.

"We could move far away from here, somewhere you'd be safe," she insisted.

I shot out of my seat, enraged. "All you ever do is run.

You've been running away from your past for ten years. I asked you earlier if you were running from something or toward something. I get it now. It's why you always kept us away from the Midwest. It's why you never let me choose where we'd go next. You knew I'd want to come back to this area because it's the only place that's ever felt like home."

Mom's eyes followed me as I paced across the living room. "Kathryn, calm down—"

"Don't you think it's time to finally face your past?" I asked bitterly.

She furrowed her brow. "What do you mean?"

I stopped abruptly. "Maybe it's time we finally talk about the night you tried to kill yourself."

The room went dead silent for ten agonizing seconds.

I took a deep breath and sat next to my mom on the couch. "Mom, there's something you should know about that night."

She fell quiet again as I told her the truth about Clinton. A wave of emotions consumed me. Hot, heavy tears rolled down my cheeks. I sniffled, but I didn't hold the tears back.

Without warning, a second wave hit, this one stronger than the last. I leaned against my mom and buried my face in her shoulder. My sobs grew audible, and my head began to hurt from the tension.

Mom pulled me tighter into her arms. Slowly, she reached out and stroked my wings.

She sighed heavily. "It's so unbelievable—"

"Mom, don't," I said, drawing away from her. "This isn't

something I made up. This isn't in my head. It's really happening."

Her expression softened. "Kathryn, I—" She paused for a moment and inhaled a deep breath. "I believe you."

I had the sudden urge to cry again, though this time for different reasons. I'd waited a long time to hear my mom to say those words. I honestly never thought I would.

For one brief moment, all seemed right in the world.

19

*I*t was impossible to sleep that night knowing that just two floors below me lay my destiny. Despite the restless sleep I had, I woke early and headed to the basement in my pajamas. I slowly ran my fingers over the carving again, trying to take in every detail.

"Grace," I whispered into thin air, "how am I supposed to get to you?"

I forced my body to relax. It took an incredible amount of effort when all I wanted to do was smash through the wall. I pictured purple energy flowing through my body and pressed my hands to the stone like I had before. Disappointment washed over me when nothing happened.

Ignoring Marek's instruction, I placed my index finger into the cavity and concentrated on sending my magic down my fingertips and into the lock. That didn't work, either.

A moment later, the doorbell rang. I quickly jerked away from the wall like I'd been caught doing something wrong. I heard my mother's muffled voice from upstairs telling me to get the door.

I didn't know what I expected, but I certainly didn't expect to find Trenton standing on my front porch. He wore a tight black t-shirt that showed off his muscular arms. His blond hair hung in loose waves around his face, and his jaw was outlined in a small amount of stubble. I'd be damned if he wasn't as hot as Marek.

I probably looked like a mess. I hadn't even brushed my hair yet; it was tied in a messy bun atop my head.

"Hey, Trenton. What are you doing here?" I asked curiously.

He smiled confidently. "I wanted to see you."

"Really?" My voice came out several pitches higher than normal.

Trenton stared at me with sexy, smoldering eyes. He spoke softly. "I can't stop thinking about you."

I was struck silent as butterflies danced around in my stomach.

"Who is it?" my mom called from her office upstairs.

"Just a friend," I yelled up to her.

I turned back to Trenton. He had this look in his eyes like he wanted to talk to me about something. I stepped outside into warm, humid air and closed the door behind me.

"What's up?" I asked.

"Here's the thing, Ryn," he said without hesitation. "I like you."

His confession came unexpectedly. I didn't know how to respond.

"I really like hanging out with you. I need to know if you feel something, too." He spoke with a hint of urgency.

I stared up into his dark brown eyes. The more I hung out with Trenton, the more I thought we could work together. But then there was Marek...

"We have fun together, and it was awesome when you stood up to Casey." Trenton reached out to gently take my hand. "Am I crazy, or is there something between us?"

I blinked several times. My hand hardly felt like my own as he ran his fingers across it.

Dammit. I had to say *something*.

Finally, I found my voice. "Trenton, we hardly know each other."

That never stopped me with Marek.

He shrugged like it didn't matter. "What do you want to know?"

"I—I don't know," I stammered. What *did* I want to know about him?

"All that matters is that we have fun together," Trenton said. "It doesn't matter that we don't know about each other's pasts."

I smiled lightly. "You say that like you don't want to talk about your past."

Trenton smirked, confirming he had secrets of his own. "Well, do you want to talk about yours?"

My mind instantly fell upon all the things I *didn't* want to talk about. My mom. Clinton. Dorian.

Trenton spoke quickly. "If you must know, my mother abandoned me because she's the polar opposite of my father; my father basically lives on another planet; and my grandma, who I lived with since I was born, died when—"

"No," I cut him off. I didn't want to have to share all my secrets, too. "I don't want to know all that. It's kind of nice being friends without having to know everything."

"You sure?" he asked with an amused smile. "Because I have plenty of secrets to share. I just need to know if…"

I suddenly felt self-conscious as he stared down at me. I couldn't explain why my cheeks heated under his gaze. "Need to know what?"

Trenton's eyes danced across my face. He reached out slowly and brushed a strand of hair out of my eyes. "I need to know if you're as amazing as you seem."

I couldn't help but smile. But as much as I enjoyed the compliments, it didn't feel right to accept them. Not when I was still hung up on Marek. Not when Grace needed me right now. Not when—

Without warning, Trenton's lips swooped down to meet mine. My entire body tensed. It took a moment for my mind to catch up and realize what was happening. Instinct took over. I relaxed into his embrace and found myself kissing him back. My heart fluttered, but it wasn't the crazy heart-pounding excitement I felt when Marek kissed me.

Trenton's lips parted to deepen the kiss. His lips weren't as soft as Marek's.

I suddenly became aware that my mind was on Marek while I was kissing Trenton. This wasn't fair to him. I drew away.

Trenton's eyes searched mine. I tried to keep my

expression neutral, to not give away my thoughts. He smiled down at me as if expecting me to tell him how amazing it was.

But I couldn't lie to him.

My small voice broke the silence. "Trenton, I'm sorry."

He furrowed his brow. "Sorry for what?"

My throat closed up around my words. I didn't want to hurt his feelings.

"I'm not sure I can handle this right now," I said.

Trenton's shoulders dropped. Shit. I was going to be the asshole who broke his heart.

"There's a lot going on in my life," I told him. "I need some time to think about it."

I couldn't watch his heart break in front of me. I did the only thing I could think to do to save us both the trouble. I turned to the door behind me and left Trenton standing on my front porch.

Great. Now I was an asshole *and* a coward.

I breathed a heavy sigh and leaned my back against the front door. I closed my eyes and listened to the stairs creak under Trenton's weight as he retreated. The sound of his car engine reached my ears, but it faded as he drove off down the street.

Tension formed in my head. *Did* I feel something for Trenton? Had I betrayed Marek by kissing him? I hated leaving him hanging like that, but I didn't know what else to do. He deserved better than me.

20

The next morning, I contemplated how to tell Allie about what happened since I last saw her. I settled on telling her about my mom first.

"I told my mom," I admitted on our way to school Monday morning.

Allie glanced to me from the driver's seat. "Really? How'd she take it?"

I pondered it for a moment. "Better than I thought. It took some convincing, but it's kind of a relief that she knows."

"I bet it was hard trying to keep it from her," she said.

I shrugged. "I never thought I'd tell her, to be honest. I didn't think she'd believe me."

"But she does, doesn't she?" Allie asked.

"Yeah. But *you're* not going to believe what else happened to me yesterday."

"Oh?" Allie's eyebrows rose curiously.

I bit the inside of my lip. "Trenton kissed me."

"*What?*" Allie's foot tapped the brakes.

"Yeah, but I'm not sure about him. It wasn't the same as kissing Marek." I knotted my hands in my lap. "Marek doesn't seem all that interested in me, though. Maybe I should give Trenton a chance. I *do* like him." It sounded like I was trying to convince myself of that.

Allie pulled into the school's parking lot. She cut the engine and turned to me. "No. Here's what you're going to do. You're going to grow a pair of balls and tell Marek you kissed Trenton."

I leaned away from her. "Whoa. When did you become the boss of me?"

"Just now," she said with a smile. "Marek likes you; I know it. Now get your butt into school and make that boy jealous."

I laughed. "And what if he doesn't care that I kissed Trenton?"

Allie shrugged. "His loss."

"Fine. I'll think about it," I said as I exited the vehicle.

Allie and I walked up to school together. We entered the front doors into the common room. My eyes instantly fell on Marek seated at one of the chairs surrounding the mansion's fireplace. Kyle sat next to him in the adjacent chair, and a group of three sophomores sat on the couch across from them. Several other students passed through the room.

Allie nudged me with her elbow.

"Right now?" I hissed under my breath.

Allie wiggled her eyebrows. "Now or never."

A smile lit up Marek's face. He turned and noticed us

for the first time. His smile widened when his eyes met mine, and my stomach summersaulted inside my abdomen.

"Hey, Kyle." Allie motioned for him to join her.

He stood, leaving me the seat beside Marek. I gladly sank into it before my legs turned to mush under Marek's sexy gaze.

"Hey," he said. "What's up?"

My eyes followed Allie and Kyle as they disappeared into the hallway behind the grand staircase. I turned back to Marek and shrugged. I wasn't about to admit everything to him with an audience.

"Did you make any progress?" he asked.

"You mean with…" I lowered my voice. "With Grace? No, I don't have any ideas."

Marek frowned. "Fletcher and I came up empty handed, too."

"Don't you think Fletcher's trying a little too hard to find an answer in his history books?" I asked.

Marek leaned an elbow on the armrest of his chair. "I don't know. He's a history teacher. That's kind of his thing."

The warning bell rang, and the three sophomores stood to head to class. Marek shifted his weight, but he didn't get to his feet when he saw I wasn't moving.

"What's up?" Marek asked.

I want you.

My heart pounded wildly in my chest. My throat closed up around my words, forcing them back down my throat.

"Nothing." I tried to sound confident in my answer, but I wasn't sure I succeeded.

"Ryn," Marek said gently. He reached out and took my fingers in his.

My breath hitched.

"Are you okay?" He sounded genuinely concerned.

An intense internal conflict sparked inside of me. I wanted nothing more than to spit out the words yet remain completely silent at the same time.

"I'm fine," I lied.

"No, you're not," he accused. "I know you."

I dropped my gaze and mumbled under my breath. "Hardly."

"Hardly?" he asked like he couldn't believe what I was saying. "Just because we haven't known each other long doesn't mean we don't know each other. I know your secrets. We spend almost all our time together."

"But you still don't want to *be* together." I was surprised to hear the words slip out of my mouth.

Marek's expression quickly turned to confusion. "Is that what's wrong?"

I couldn't bear to look at him. "I—I guess so."

Marek squeezed my hand tighter to get me to look at him. "You can't honestly think I don't want to be with you, Ryn."

Suddenly, the words didn't seem so difficult to find anymore. "Of course I think that. Why would I think otherwise? You've given no indication that you want to be more than friends. Not since we kissed. And I thought that meant something."

"It did," Marek insisted. "It meant something. Every moment I've spent with you has meant something."

I wanted to believe his words, but his actions showed otherwise. "Then why haven't you shown it?"

Marek dropped my hand and raked his fingers through his hair while I spoke.

"Why haven't you done anything?" I asked. "Why—"

"Why haven't *you*?" he shouted.

Two students climbing the stairs gave him a strange look.

Marek seemed just as shocked as I was at his question. He rubbed his hand over his face before dropping it to his lap.

I waited until the common room was empty again before speaking. I didn't care that we only had a minute left to get to class.

"I thought it was obvious," I whispered.

In one swift motion, Marek rose to his feet and pulled me up to stand beside him. Our bodies nearly touched as he tucked a strand of loose hair behind my ear. He closed his eyes and rested his forehead against mine. He smelled familiar—like leather and clean laundry.

For one long moment, it felt as if the world had stopped. My heart rose in my chest, and my breath stopped. We stood frozen, like we were suspended in time.

All too soon, time started again. My heart dropped back down where it belonged and hammered against my rib cage. My breath returned in an uncontrollable, shallow rhythm.

"I'm so sorry, Ryn," Marek whispered.

My knees quivered as his hot breath rushed across my face.

"For what?" I asked in a shaky voice. Now that he was this close to me, it didn't seem like he should be apologizing for anything.

"For leading you on and then just leaving you to read the rest of the signals yourself."

"There were signals?" If it wasn't for my quiet, breathy voice, I was sure the question would've shattered the entire tone of the moment. Somehow, it didn't.

Marek's blue eyes opened and focused on me. "Of course there were. I want to be with you. I just didn't think we should right now, not with everything going on. You needed to focus on your training, not on me."

"And you thought ignoring the topic would accomplish that? If you don't claim me, Marek, someone else will. Trenton kissed me."

Marek's expression hardened. "He did?"

I nodded sheepishly.

"I never meant to let you think I wasn't interested," Marek said. "It was Fletcher's fault. He insisted I leave you alone."

I let out a breath of disbelief. *That jerk.*

"But he lets us train together," I said.

Marek nodded. "He wanted to train you himself, but I talked him into letting me help. He said I could only if I didn't distract you."

I thought about all the times he'd pulled me close during our training sessions. "You didn't make that very easy. You, James Marek, are pretty damn distracting."

Marek brushed his fingers through the ends of my hair. "So are you, Ryn."

Marek bent to brush his lips against mine. Shock riveted through me before I could really process what was happening. One taste wasn't enough for either of us. His arms wrapped around my waist, pulling me into an embrace. His lips pressed against mine with a passion I'd never felt before.

Everything else around us vanished. Even the hardwood floor seemed to evaporate from beneath us. He kissed me like nothing else in this world mattered. Heat rose to every inch of my skin as my body pressed harder against his. I clung to him, never wanting to let go.

Disappointment washed over me when he drew away. I was glad he kept his hands on my shoulders or I might've fallen over from the spell he'd put on me.

"Now do you believe me?" Marek asked.

I answered with a wide grin.

In the heat of the moment, I forgot we were standing in the common room. Marek's face fell as his eyes locked on something—*someone*—behind me.

My stomach dropped to the floor when I turned to find Trenton standing at the base of the staircase. He glared at us with a deeply hurt expression on his face.

Shit. I'd just graduated far, *far* beyond asshole.

"Trenton, wait," I said.

He was already quickly retreating down the hall.

"I'm sorry," I called after him.

The problem was, I wasn't sure that was true.

"I can't believe this!" I complained to Allie after school in her bedroom. "Can I see your pillow? I'd like to scream into it."

Allie smiled in amusement and tossed her pillow across the bed at me. I pulled it to my face and screamed, more for show than anything.

"Are you okay?" Allie asked in genuine concern.

I placed the pillow between me and the wall and leaned against it. "I'm overwhelmed. I just broke a guy's heart, and I actually kind of liked him. I've found Grace but can't get to her. Should I go on?"

"We'll get to her," Allie assured me confidently. "We just need to find the key."

I glanced at her skeptically.

"I mean it," she said. "Your instinct led you to Grace. It should lead you to the key, too."

I frowned. "You keep saying things like that, but I don't feel anything."

"Maybe the key is in your house somewhere," she suggested.

"Yeah," I said sarcastically. "Maybe the owners left it on the kitchen counter. I must've missed it when we moved in."

Allie hopped up from her bed and bent to slip her tennis shoes on. "I know what you need."

I eyed her. "What's that?"

"A break," she said.

"No," I objected. "I've already spent enough time distracted today. Between school and practicing my essence with Marek, I hardly had a moment to put more thought into Grace."

"You thought about it *all* day yesterday," Allie pointed out. "Just take a deep breath, okay?"

I reluctantly followed her instruction, but it didn't help. Instead, I shoved my head into her pillow and screamed again. That helped some.

Allie laughed at me.

"Fine," I agreed. "We can take a *short* break."

Allie grabbed her purse. "Let's get something to eat."

On the way to Angela's Café, I noticed for the first time how little I'd eaten over the past two days. I had a ham sandwich earlier that day at lunch. Besides that, I wasn't sure of the last time I ate. I ordered an extra side of potato salad to help fill my belly. My stress eased slightly once we finished eating—though my wallet wasn't pleased.

There was a chill in the air when we stepped outside after our meal. I glanced up the street and noticed Celeste's next door. I had the sudden urge to go inside and check it out.

"Hey." I caught Allie's attention. "Didn't you say you wanted to take me here sometime?"

Allie looked toward the small jewelry shop. "Yeah. You love earrings so much, I thought you'd like it."

I absentmindedly twirled the green studs around in my ears. "Let's check it out."

Allie pulled open the door to Celeste's, and we stepped inside. It was like walking straight into heaven. Unique handcrafted pieces of jewelry hung from the displays. Every necklace I walked by was different from the last. Beautiful stones and gorgeous beads filled my senses, and I caught a hint of rose in the air. The place was perfect.

My eyes fell upon a display of earrings. I rushed over to it.

"I like these ones!" I held up a pair of earrings that dangled with small white feathers.

Allie inhaled a sharp breath. "You should make your own!"

Excitement filled me. I lowered my voice to a whisper even though we were alone. "You mean, from my *own* wings? That is probably the best idea I've ever heard."

"Do you have the supplies? Because if you don't, I think they have jewelry-making kits over there." She pointed.

"Making jewelry sounds like fun." I grabbed two more sets of earrings and contemplated spending the money on them.

"Come on." Allie led me down the aisle.

I eyed the array of earring hooks, trying to decide on a color.

"Do you ladies need any help?" a woman's voice came from behind us.

I turned to find a thin woman just a few years older than me standing close by. She had long, straight brown hair and a friendly smile. She wore a lot of jewelry, but in a tasteful way. Several rings adorned her fingers, and her ears had been double pierced. A necklace with a key pendant on it hung around her neck.

"No, thank you." I smiled back.

"Okay," she said. "My name's Meg. Let me know if you change your mind. We close in a few minutes, but you're free to browse as long as you like."

"Thank you." I turned back to the hooks and opted for the silver ones. I grabbed one of the jewelry-making kits from the bottom shelf.

Allie and I continued down the row slowly. I couldn't help but take in every piece of jewelry I laid eyes on.

"I swear I could spend a whole week in this store and not get bored," I said. "Oh, look. More earrings!"

By the time we finished browsing the aisles, I'd settled on three pairs of earrings and the supplies needed to make my own. It would eat up the rest of my birthday money, but I'd been saving it for something good.

"All set?" Meg asked cheerfully when we reached the counter.

"Yep," Allie answered for the both of us. She handed over a pretty blue stone necklace for Meg to ring up.

"Do you wear a lot of jewelry?" Meg asked to keep up the small talk.

Allie gestured to me. "She collects earrings."

"Ooh." Meg seemed suddenly interested. "Have any favorite styles?"

I shrugged. "Depends on my mood. I like studs, but if I'm going for cute, I'll try anything unique and dangly."

Meg wiggled her eyebrows. "Anyone you're trying to look cute *for*?" She took Allie's cash from her hand and opened the register.

My gaze dropped slightly as a blush rose to my cheeks. "There's this guy—"

I froze when my eyes fell on Meg's necklace. She didn't seem to notice my words had instantly stopped in their tracks.

"What's he like?" Meg asked.

I hardly processed the sound of her voice over my own pulse pounding in my ears. At first, Meg's necklace had seemed ordinary, like the key had been made to be a necklace—but I knew it had a far greater purpose. It looked old, unlike any car or house key I'd ever owned. I couldn't take my eyes off the angel wing design that spread out at the end of the key.

The key matched the exact pattern of the Davina wings carved into my basement wall.

22

Meg caught me staring.

"Sorry," I said breathlessly when my eyes met hers. "I like your necklace. Do you have any more like it?"

Meg handed Allie her receipt and then touched her fingers lightly to the key. "Unfortunately, I don't. Most of our jewelry is hand crafted with things we find at flea markets. We aim to make every piece unique."

I swallowed hard, still not sure if I'd breathed at all in the last minute. "What about yours? Did that key come from a flea market?"

"No. My grandpa gave it to me before he passed. My grandma said it'd been in the family for generations, but I never found out what it went to. I figure whatever it unlocked is long gone. It makes a great necklace, though, doesn't it?"

"Yeah, it does," I said flatly. "I guess that means it's not for sale."

Meg frowned. "It's not. But we can keep an eye out for something similar if you'd like and make you a custom piece."

"No," I said. "It's just... I think I might know what it opens."

Meg placed a protective hand over the key. Her voice became defensive. "Like I said, it's not for sale."

Meg rang up my total, but each passing moment felt like an eternity. I barely remembered handing over my money. It wasn't until Allie and I stepped outside, still keyless, that I had a moment to let it all sink in.

"Oh my gosh!" Allie burst with excitement. She hopped up and down as we took a few steps down the sidewalk.

Shock hit me so hard that I had to stop and lean myself against the outside of Angela's Café. My head swam, and my heart raced.

"I was right," Allie gloated, still jumping around ecstatically. "I *told* you that your magic would lead you to the key, and it did. It led you to Celeste's just like it led you to Grace!"

"Shh..." I glanced up and down the street, but no one was nearby to overhear. "Okay, lesson learned. Never question my instinct again, especially when it comes to Grace. I just want to know how we're going to get our hands on that key."

Allie calmed down and leaned against the building beside me. "I don't know. Maybe we could talk to her and tell her why we need it."

"Great idea." I rolled my eyes. "What are we supposed to say? 'Hey, there's an ancient angel buried in my basement. I have the power to wake her and save the world from impending doom. The only thing holding us back is that we need a key to get to her, and you have it.' If you want to go back into the jewelry shop to say all that, be my guest."

"Maybe don't word it like *that*. But if that key has been in her family for generations, she's probably a Davina. She'd know the stories. I'm sure she'd be willing to help."

I pushed myself away from the wall. "I don't know, Allie."

"We could—" she started, but she abruptly stopped when the sound of familiar voices hit our ears.

The door to Angela's Café opened, and Casey stepped out, laughing. Troy and Trenton followed behind her. Trenton's expression immediately fell when he saw me, and I stiffened.

Casey's laughter died, and a look of disgust crossed her face. She took her time eyeing Allie and me up and down individually. I saw it as a blessing that she continued down the sidewalk without saying a word, but the tension in the air was practically suffocating.

Trenton's eyes caught mine as he passed. He scowled.

I wanted to say something to him—to apologize—but I couldn't find the words. He was too far down the sidewalk by the time I found the courage to open my mouth.

"Is it just me, or did it seem like Casey was trying to kill us with her stare?" Allie asked once they were out of earshot.

"Definitely trying to kill us. She knows we're going to beat them in our first mock battle."

"I don't think that's why she was looking at us like that."

I tore my gaze from Casey's retreating figure as she ducked her head into a vehicle. "What's your theory, then?"

"I know why she hates me. The question is, why was she looking at *you* like that?"

I ignored her question. "Why *does* she hate you?"

"I asked you first," Allie challenged.

"I'll tell you if you tell me."

"Fine," Allie agreed. "I'll tell you in the car."

After getting into her car, we sat silently for what felt like a full minute. Allie didn't make a move to start the vehicle, but her hands gripped the steering wheel tightly.

"Okay," she breathed, like telling the story was hard for her. "Something you might not know is that Casey and I used to be really good friends."

"Really?" I asked in shock.

"I know," she agreed. "It seems so unlikely now, but people change. We were practically inseparable until high school."

"What happened?" I asked, dreading the answer.

"Well, for one, puberty hit," Allie said with a tense laugh. "Casey had always been—how do I put this?—bossy. I never really thought much about it. It was just the way she was. Casey was pretty and popular, and if you wanted to be Casey's friend, you did whatever Casey said."

"So," I teased, "she hasn't changed much?"

Allie gave an uncomfortable smile and then continued her story. "Basically, being friends with her was toxic, and it only got worse in junior high."

"In what way?" I asked curiously.

Allie shrugged. "Little things all piling up. She'd tell me

I was ugly or dumb or whatever, but then the next day she was all about how pretty and smart I was."

Allie's story reminded me of a friend I'd made in eighth grade. Needless to say, I was grateful to move away from *that* school.

"According to Casey, I could never do anything right, and no matter what I did, she was always *better* at it."

I couldn't help but feel sorry for Allie. "Why'd you stay friends with her?"

A shamed expression crossed her face. "I don't know. I guess I thought our friendship meant something. Then the summer between junior high and high school happened." She took a deep breath. "By the time we started at Galen High, our friendship was over for good."

I waited for her to elaborate, but she'd gone silent.

"What happened that summer?" I prodded.

"It sounds dumb now that I think about it, but it was, like, the biggest deal in the world back then. I fell *really* hard for this guy we used to go to school with."

I could already see where this was going. "Do I know him?"

Allie shook her head. "We went to junior high together, but not high school. He went to Eagle Valley High and graduated last year. He wasn't a Davina."

It was hard to picture Allie having a crush on anyone besides Kyle.

"Anyway, Blake and I—that was his name—spent a lot of the summer talking online. And, of course, I gushed every detail of it to Casey. Then suddenly, *she* liked him, too."

"Ugh, that's the worst," I said.

Allie scowled. "I haven't gotten to the good part yet. Obviously, it annoyed me that she liked him, but I still stayed friends with her. Don't ask me why. But Blake didn't like Casey. When we hung out with him, he didn't really show any interest in her even though she flirted like crazy."

"Good. You're worth way more than she is."

"Thanks," she said sheepishly. "I'd never really had anyone show interest in me because they were always falling all over Casey."

"Boys are stupid," I said. "You're twice as pretty with ten times the personality."

Allie forced a smile. "Thanks. Anyway, since Blake didn't go for her, I thought we had something special. But then I started noticing that he wasn't talking to me online as much. He always seemed to take forever to respond back. Eventually, he told me that he didn't know how he felt about me because he thought he might be falling for someone else."

I drew in a sharp breath. "He did *not* have a crush on Casey."

Allie dropped her gaze. "Well, not exactly…"

"Oh, she *did not*," I said, suddenly catching on.

"She did. She created a fake profile and started talking to him just so he'd stop paying attention to me."

"I'm *so* glad you stopped being friends with her. That's unforgiveable."

"The part that sucks is that the fake profile she made basically *was* me. This fake girl liked all the same music as me, read all the same books I read, even had dark black hair like I do. Casey would steal my statuses and reword them. Like, if I was upset, her fake persona was upset. If I was having a good day, this fake girl was having a good day. It's like she was trying to *be* me in order to get Blake's attention."

"But he wasn't really paying attention to *her*," I pointed out.

"But to Casey, he was. And by that point, she'd distracted him enough that he stopped caring about me. I'm sure that's all she wanted."

"What a *bitch*," I muttered under my breath.

Allie raised her eyebrows. "And you didn't believe me the first time I told you that."

"It wasn't about believing you. I just thought you were being a bit harsh. But now I'm not sure that word does the girl justice."

"I expected better from a friend," Allie said. "I expect better from a *Davina*."

Her words hung in the air for several long seconds.

"So, how'd you find out it was her?" I asked.

Allie's grip tightened around the steering wheel. "She admitted it to me. We were still friends, and I was telling her all about this girl that Blake said he liked. She started laughing and told me *she* was behind the account. She even logged into it on her computer to show me and then bragged about how often they talked."

"I hope you smashed that computer," I said.

Allie smiled. "No, but I did walk out of her house, and I never came back."

"I'm proud of you," I told her. "Casey doesn't deserve a friend like you."

"Thanks. I hate that it took me so long to realize it." She let out a breath and looked at me expectantly. "So, that's my story. What about yours?"

I hated how quickly the conversation changed topics. Quietness settled over the car for several moments.

Finally, I lifted my gaze. "First of all, Casey doesn't like me because I hang out with you and Marek. I think that automatically earns me a spot on her hit list."

"But there's more," Allie said with certainty.

"I should've told you about it sooner, but I thought I'd get in trouble if anyone knew."

The confusion on Allie's face deepened. "What happened?"

I remained silent and chewed on my bottom lip.

"Ryn, nothing you say to me is going to get you in trouble. I'm good at keeping secrets." She paused for a moment. "Unless you think I'll judge you for it… Ryn, I'm not—"

"No, I don't think that," I said quickly. "Honestly, you'll probably be proud of me."

Allie's confusion morphed into curiosity. "Now you *have* to tell me."

I couldn't help the grin that spread over my face. "It's nothing, really. I just… kind of… threatened Casey with a fireball."

"What?" Allie asked like she hadn't heard me correctly.

"Yeah, just over there." I pointed to the front of Celeste's. "It was last Friday, the night Trenton and I went out to dinner. We ran into Casey afterward, and she was being her usual self, and—"

I stopped abruptly when I turned and saw the look on Allie's face. Her jaw had dropped, and her eyes had gone wide.

My face flushed. "I know it was in public and we're supposed to keep all this stuff secret, but Trenton convinced her not to tell on me."

Allie was still frozen in shock.

"You're not mad at me, are you? You know, for showing my magic in public? I know it's risky. A couple people saw, but I don't think they—"

"Are you kidding me?" She reached out to swat me lightly. "I'm not going to tell anyone! I'm freaking *proud* of you for standing up to her."

"But it was in the middle of the street. I really should've controlled my temper."

"Don't worry about it," Allie said. "Casey probably needed that. Explains why she didn't say anything earlier. Probably afraid you'd pull another one on her."

I raised my eyebrows. "If I would've known why you guys hate each other, I might not have been able to hold back this time."

Allie laughed from beside me.

I crossed my arms and feigned disappointment. "At least you get to have fun and try to stun her. I'm thinking I'll sit out of the mock battle. I mean, I'd love to punch that girl in the face, but I don't think my magic is ready."

"You can still participate," Allie argued. "Just don't use your essence. You can practice your hand-to-hand skills."

I shot her a light smile.

"Hey, would you want to do some practice with me? You've been spending all your time training with Marek. Maybe you should shake things up."

"Oh, Allie, that's sweet, but..." How did I tell her she sucked at teaching?

"We'll only spar," she clarified.

I nodded. "Yeah, I think it might help. I'm getting used to Marek's tactics anyway. It'll help to mix things up a bit."

Her face lit up.

"But before we do, we should call Fletcher and tell him about the key," I said.

"Right. The key." Allie pulled out her phone. "Think Fletcher will have any ideas about that one?"

"I hope so," I said. "Because short of stealing it, I don't know how we're going to get our hands on it."

Fletcher sounded proud that we'd found the key so soon. Allie put him on speaker phone and set the phone between us on the middle console.

"I knew you could do it," he said. "You've been touched by Grace, Ryn, and she's going to guide you where you need to go."

"Yeah." Irritation entered my tone. "But just because we *found* the key doesn't mean we *have* it."

Fletcher went silent for a few seconds like he was considering this. "Perhaps it's best if I come along with you to talk to her."

"I think Celeste's already closed today," Allie pointed out.

I followed her gaze past the passenger side window and to the jewelry shop. The open sign that'd been lit when we arrived had been turned off. "Well, that sucks."

"We can try talking to her tomorrow," Fletcher suggested.

I had a feeling getting ahold of the key wouldn't be as easy as he made it sound.

"Did you hear what happened?" Allie spoke so quickly the following morning that I barely understood her.

I dropped my backpack onto the floor of her car and slid into the passenger seat. "What?"

"Someone broke into Celeste's. The front window is broken and everything. You should pay more attention to social media. Here."

Allie handed me her phone as she drove.

"Social media is just filled with people from my old schools who I don't care about and who probably don't even remember who I am." In other words, it was a total waste of my time.

I glanced down at Allie's screen. She'd pulled up a picture of the jewelry shop. The displays in the window looked the same as they had yesterday, but the glass on the front door had been shattered. I quickly scanned through the description that went with it. According to the post, the shop had been broken into late last night. Though some of the merchandise had been rummaged through, they had no evidence to suggest that anything of value had been taken.

"Oh my God!" I exclaimed when I finished reading the post. "Who would *do* that?"

"I don't know," Allie said.

"Aren't there cameras or something? They'll catch the person who did it, won't they?"

Allie raised her eyebrows. "Are you kidding me? Do you *realize* how small of a town this is?"

"Do *you* realize we live in a world where cameras are everywhere? Even if the jewelry shop doesn't have cameras, there must be *some* nearby looking out onto the street. Maybe someone saw something. Like you said, it's a small town. Gossip spreads fast."

"The police report made it sound like they were pretty clueless," Allie said. "If any cameras caught the guy, he was probably disguised or something."

I handed her phone back. "We're assuming it's a he?"

Allie pulled into the school's parking lot. "I was just saying that in general." She turned off the engine but didn't get out of the car. "Don't you think it's a little weird?"

"What? A break-in in Eagle Valley? Yeah, I suppose."

"I mean isn't it weird that they didn't take anything. Like, sure, it's just a cute shop and they're not selling engagement rings or anything like that, but wouldn't you think that if someone went through all that trouble to break in that they'd at least head for the cash register or something?"

"Well, yeah, I suppose. What are you getting at, Allie?"

"What if they were looking for something that wasn't there?"

"You think this has something to do with the key?" I asked.

"I think it has everything to do with the key."

Even though school was going to start in a few minutes, I felt rooted to my seat.

"That doesn't make any sense," I said. "Why now? And why not break into Meg's house instead of the shop?"

Allie glanced around the parking lot. "What if someone overheard us talking about it? Did we mention Meg had the key, or were we just talking about how it was in the shop?"

I went completely silent, but my heart beat rapidly against my rib cage.

"How could someone have overheard us? We were in your car practically the whole time." My eyes darted around the vehicle. "This thing isn't bugged, is it?"

Allie looked at me like I was being stupid. Apparently, my question didn't even dignify a response.

"*Practically* is the key word there," she said. "We mentioned the key as soon as we stepped out of the shop."

"But there wasn't anyone on the street."

Allie bit her lip. "I don't know. Maybe I'm just being paranoid. Maybe it has nothing to do with the key."

I suddenly felt sympathetic for her. "Well, I think you're right to be cautious. I still think we should go over there after school and try to talk to Meg. Maybe the break-in will actually help our case."

"How?" Allie looked surprised.

"If someone's after the key, maybe she'll help us."

Allie twisted her lips in thought. "If they didn't get to her first."

~

"Please tell me I'm making progress," I pleaded with Marek during second period.

Fletcher had paired us up for sparring in the valley again. I was well aware I was distracted today.

"You're doing better," Marek admitted. "I think the extra practice after school has been helping."

I threw a punch in his direction, which he swiftly dodged. "I'm going to have to skip out today."

"Why?" Marek swung his leg around to knock me off my feet.

I landed on my back with a hard thud. He was on top of me a second later, pinning my arms to my sides with his knees. I didn't even try to fight back. Marek stared down at me with desire in his eyes. If we weren't in the middle of class, I'd have kissed him already.

He seemed to notice he'd been on top of me a moment too long. He rolled off of me and got to his feet.

I sat up. "Did Allie tell you what happened yesterday?"

Marek held out a hand to help me up. "Most of it, I think."

"Then you know we have to go back and talk to the girl from the jewelry shop about the key."

"Yeah," Marek said. "And I'm coming with."

"You are?"

"You and Allie are the ones having all the fun lately, searching for Grace and now the key." He looked genuinely disappointed.

"Yeah, but you get to have fun training me every day," I teased. "That's an important job."

"Don't flatter yourself," he laughed.

I told myself he wanted to come because he wanted to spend more time with me. It made the rest of the day bearable, but by the time the final bell rang that day, I wasn't sure what to expect once we went to talk to Meg.

When we reached Celeste's after school, it looked different from the picture I'd seen that morning. The glass had been cleaned up, and two men stood near the open door installing a brand new pane.

Allie and I stepped out of her car. Marek had followed along on his motorcycle, and Fletcher in his own vehicle.

The two men nodded a greeting to the four of us as we approached the door. Inside, a middle-aged woman stood behind the counter and talked to a man dressed in a polo shirt and nice slacks. I heard him call the woman *Celeste* and realized she was the owner. By the look of the logo on the guy's shirt, I guessed he was there to install a new security system. A few displays had been moved since yesterday. I shuttered to think what the place looked like before they'd spent all day cleaning it up.

Celeste looked up when we entered. "I'm sorry. We're closed today."

Fletcher stepped to the front of the group. "We're not here to browse. We're looking for Meg. Is she around?"

Celeste frowned. "I'm afraid not. She's a little shook up about what happened last night. Do you know her well?"

"No," Fletcher admitted, "but we wanted to offer our sympathies."

She smiled lightly. "Thank you, but you'll have to visit her at home."

"Do you happen to know where she lives?" Fletcher asked.

Celeste narrowed her eyes. "I'm not allowed to give out that type of information about our employees. If you don't know her that well, I'm sure it can wait. I can let her know you stopped in, though."

Fletcher leaned up against the front counter casually. Casual didn't work well for him. If he was trying to charm her, he should've left that job to Marek.

"Can't you make an exception this one time?" Fletcher asked softly.

"What did you say your name was?" Celeste's tone was harsh.

"Please," I begged, stepping forward. "My friend and I were in here yesterday just before the shop closed. We know Meg was working and closed up just hours before the break-in. All we want is to check on her."

Celeste eyed me. I must've come across as more trustworthy than Fletcher because she relaxed.

"You were here yesterday?" she asked.

"Yeah," I said.

"You didn't see anything suspicious, did you? No one hanging around or anything?"

My shoulders dropped. "No. The break-in was during the middle of the night, wasn't it?"

"Yes, but it never hurts to ask," Celeste said.

"Did they take anything?" I hoped she'd say yes. I *really* didn't want this to be about the key.

Celeste's brow furrowed. "No, and that's the strange part. I'm not sure they were looking for something of value. I think it was just a simple case of vandalism. My guess is some teenagers playing a prank."

"Do the police have any idea who did it?" I asked.

Her voice grew more irritated, but I couldn't blame her. This had to be a stressful day for her, and people had probably been asking the same questions all day. "Unfortunately, the public knows just about as much as I do. No suspects have been identified yet. I do appreciate you coming in to check on Meg. It was very nice of you."

It was clear in her tone that was the end of the conversation.

"Would you be able to get her a message if I left it with you?" I asked.

"Sure," she said flatly. She glanced around behind the counter and handed me a blank piece of paper and a pen.

I paused for a moment, unsure of what to say. Feeling like I was taking too long, I quickly jotted down the only thing I could think of.

Meg,

The Davina need your help. Please call me as soon as you can.

-The girl who liked your necklace

I wrote my phone number at the bottom then folded the paper into a small square and added Meg's name to the outside.

"We're sorry to bother you," I told Celeste genuinely as I slid the paper across the counter. "Thank you so much."

I could sense everyone's disappointment hit simultaneously when we exited the shop. The unspoken question hung in the air. *What do we do now?*

"I'll poke around on social media," Allie offered. "I'll see if I can find out Meg's last name so we can track her down and talk to her."

"I'll call a few people and see if anyone knows her personally," Fletcher offered.

"I can't believe we were so close!" I complained. "We're better off blasting through that wall than waiting around."

"I don't think that's a good idea." Marek meant it like a suggestion, but it sounded like a subtle demand.

"If something doesn't happen soon, you're not going to be able to stop me," I said.

Marek smiled. "I'd like to see you try."

"How would you stop me? Are you going to start stalking me?" I actually didn't think I'd mind if he did.

"Let's start with making up that training session we missed today," Marek suggested.

I crossed my arms over my chest. "Does it even matter at this point?"

"Yes," Fletcher answered immediately.

"I should be doing something to get that key," I insisted.

"Allie and I can handle that," Fletcher said. "Your training is just as important."

"Why?" I asked. "Once I get to Grace, she can take over from there."

"Only if you manage to wake her first," Fletcher said. "To do that, you need to be able to control your essence."

I opened my mouth to argue further, but Fletcher was right. If I couldn't control my essence to wake Grace, the rest of this didn't matter.

A minute later, I had a helmet strapped to my head and was climbing onto the back of Marek's motorcycle.

Marek pulled into the parking lot behind the school. I slipped off the bike and removed the helmet. He started toward the trailhead.

I glanced toward the school. "What about the basement?"

"We'll get there. I thought we could warm up with a little flying first."

"That sounds like fun!"

Marek stopped abruptly before we made it past the edge of the school. I nearly ran into him.

"What?" I asked in alarm.

He began digging inside his pockets. "I lost my keys."

"You *just* had them on your bike."

"I must've dropped them," he said. "Give me a minute. I'll catch up with you."

Marek jogged back to the parking lot while I continued toward the trail.

Disappointment hit me when I caught the sound of a familiar voice in the distance. Casey's blond hair swayed behind her near the trailhead. Like usual, she was followed by Troy and Trenton. This time, three other people had joined them. Casey turned for a moment. I could've sworn that even from this distance her eyes met mine.

"Maybe this won't be fun," I mumbled to myself.

I continued on and followed her group into the trees. I wasn't about to let her scare me off. I stared down at my feet as I walked, my thoughts racing. Maybe flying would help clear my mind.

The sound of a stick breaking caught my attention. I immediately froze. Before I had a chance to assess my surroundings, a hard object hit my chest and stole the air from my lungs. The ground swayed beneath my feet, and everything went dark.

"Are you okay?" The voice sounded like it was coming from under water. Strong hands shook my shoulders. "Are you okay?" the voice repeated, this time coming across more clearly.

I opened my eyes and blinked a few times until Marek's face came into focus.

"What?" I sat up. "What just happened?"

Marek scanned the trees. "You were stunned."

I suddenly felt more alert. "What the hell? Who would do that?"

"I don't know." Marek still didn't take his eyes off the forest. "I could've sworn…"

"Sworn what?" I pushed myself to my feet and dusted the dirt off my jeans.

Marek finally looked at me. "I'm not sure what I saw. I just made it to the entrance of the trail when you fell."

"Did you see anyone?" I squeaked.

Marek squinted into the trees again. "I saw movement, but I couldn't make him out. I threw essence at him, but I missed."

"Is this someone's idea of a joke?" I raised my voice and projected it into the trees. "It's not funny!"

I pushed past Marek and started toward the parking lot. "Forget it. I thought this place was supposed to be safe now."

Marek seemed confused for a moment and then hurried to catch up with me. "It *should* be. I mean, we got rid of Dorian. People are coming and going from the valley all the time now that school's started."

A thought suddenly occurred to me, and I stopped in my tracks. "You don't think it was one of them, do you?"

"One of who?"

"One of the people coming and going all the time! I just saw Casey and her group headed down here."

"You're not suggesting Casey stunned you, are you?"

I gritted my teeth and continued down the trail. "I wouldn't put it past her."

Marek and I emerged from the forest.

"Why would she do that?" He sounded skeptical.

"I don't know. To show me up. To scare me."

"Casey knows the rules. We're not supposed to stun people outside of battles."

"Just because she knows the rules doesn't mean she's not above breaking them," I said. "I kind of pissed her off the other day."

"What'd you do?" He sounded genuinely curious.

I glanced around. Although no one was nearby to over-hear, I didn't feel comfortable opening up to him here.

"Can we just get out of here?" I suggested.

"Yeah, sure," he said softly. "Where do you want to go?"

"I don't know. Somewhere where I'm *not* being attacked on a daily basis."

At this point, I was pretty certain I was going to die in those woods.

He glanced behind us once. "Yeah, come on."

Marek took my hand, sending my heart fluttering. A minute later, we were speeding down the street. I felt safer once my arms were wrapped around him.

Marek stopped along the shoulder of the road outside of town. I recognized the pile of rocks that cut through the trees and climbed the hill to our left. He'd taken me here a few weeks ago. It was where we shared our first kiss.

I stepped onto the gravel shoulder and handed him the bike helmet he made me wear. "Thanks for taking me here."

Marek swung his leg over the seat and stood on the road beside me. He took my hand in his and stared down at me. "You like it here?"

I nodded. I liked being anywhere Marek was.

He didn't let go of my hand as we made our way across the road and up the hill. This time, I had a better idea of where to put my feet, so we made it to the top faster.

Marek still hadn't dropped my hand when we lowered ourselves to the rocky hilltop and looked out over Eagle Valley. Silence settled as he traced his thumb across the back of my hand.

"I'm sorry about what happened," he said quietly. "I shouldn't have left you for even a second."

"You couldn't have known some idiot was going to attack me—again. What's up with this place?"

"Maybe it comes with being chosen by Grace," Marek suggested like it was supposed to make me feel better.

I stared down at our entwined fingers. "Maybe I don't *want* to be chosen."

"I don't think you have a choice."

It didn't seem like I had a choice in anything lately. I didn't say anything.

Marek finally broke the silence. "You don't really think Casey stunned you, do you? What'd you do to make her mad?"

I sighed heavily. "If I tell you, I don't want any lectures about how stupid I was being, okay? I already know what I did wasn't cool."

"Okay," Marek agreed.

I told him about how I'd threatened Casey. It looked as if agreeing to not pass judgement was causing him physical pain. Knowing him, it took all his strength not to lecture me about using my essence in public.

"I know." I covered my face with my hands. "I was being stupid."

"Hey," Marek said softly. He placed an arm around my

shoulder and pulled me into his chest. Somehow he had the power to relax me at the smallest touch. "You're making a bigger deal out of this than it needs to be."

I dropped my hands. "You think so?"

He squeezed me tighter for reassurance.

"But what if Casey thought it was a big deal?" I asked.

"I don't know if that has anything to do with what just happened. I thought I saw someone in the woods, but it didn't look like Casey."

"I thought you said you didn't know what you saw. She could've hung back and waited around for me."

Marek fell silent. I could hear his heartbeat from where my head rested on his shoulder. I closed my eyes and pretended for a moment that everything was normal, that I'd never learned about Grace or the Davina and that I'd come to Eagle Valley to only find romance. Marek shifted, pulling me out of my daydream.

"I don't know what to think," I said quietly. "If it *was* Casey, screw her."

"And if it wasn't?" Marek asked.

"If it wasn't her, who would it be? No one else hates me enough, and it's not like I have a demon after me again." A sudden thought occurred to me, and a sharp breath passed my lips. I straightened up. "What if *she's* after me because of the key? Allie and I thought someone might've over-heard us yesterday. It was Casey. It had to be. She was right inside Angela's Café when Allie and I were talking about it."

"Whoa, slow down," he insisted.

I hadn't realized how fast I'd been talking.

"You think whoever stunned you in the woods just now is the same person who broke into Celeste's?"

"Yeah," I said slowly. I mean, there was no guarantee the break-in had anything to do with me, but it seemed like too much of a coincidence to ignore.

"And you think Casey did it?" Marek didn't sound convinced.

"Are you defending her? I thought you didn't like her."

"I'm not saying I like her. It's just, Ryn, she's a Davina."

"That doesn't mean she can be trusted," I pointed out. "Even Fletcher doesn't trust all the Davina."

"Why would she break into the jewelry shop?"

"I don't know." I honestly didn't. "Maybe she wants to find Grace herself. Or maybe she just can't stand the idea of someone else being the hero."

"But by doing that she'd unleash an army of demons into this realm. Even Casey isn't that stupid."

I pressed my lips together in thought. "But she was there both times, Marek. She must've heard us talking about Grace and the key. And she was in the woods just now. Isn't that a little suspicious?"

Marek and I couldn't seem to come to an agreement over what had been going on these last few days. He tried convincing me that the two incidents weren't related and that I was being paranoid.

All I wanted to do was kiss him to shut him up.

He wrapped me in his arms again. I felt protected and comfortable there, as if nothing could get to me as long as he was nearby. A serene silence settled over the hill. I closed my eyes and focused on the rise and fall of Marek's chest and the warmth of his arms around me.

"Marek," I said softly.

"Yeah?" he asked into my hair.

I didn't know what to say. All I wanted was to enjoy his company.

"What do you want to do with your life?" My voice came out dreamily. The light breeze was putting me to sleep.

"I want to become a Protector."

"Do you feel pressured into it?" I asked curiously.

"No. I didn't grow up with all this. I would've chosen to become a Protector anyway."

"Why's that?"

Marek pulled me closer. "I like the idea of saving people from the evil in this world."

It sounded like there was more behind his words than he was willing to admit.

"You say that like the demons aren't the only evil," I said, still half asleep.

"They're not," he stated flatly.

"What do you mean?" I listened to his heartbeat as I waited for his answer.

He finally spoke in a whisper. "I've seen evil come from other places. Maybe someday I'll tell you about it."

It was clear in his tone that today wasn't that day. I urged to ask him more, to prod for answers, but I held my tongue. I had to respect his secrets and let him come to me at his own pace. He'd do the same for me if I asked him to.

"Can the Davina be evil?" I asked.

He rested his head against mine. "I like to think the Davina are all good, but there's nothing stopping them from doing bad things."

"That makes sense," I said. "Marek?"

"Yeah?"

"I'm glad you want to protect people. You're going to be really good at it."

"Thank you," he whispered.

I remained in his arms for another hour. Unfortunately, the sun began to fall beneath the horizon, and Marek suggested it was time to take me home. Chilly air filled the empty space between us when he pulled away. Disappointment washed over me.

Fifteen minutes later, Marek walked me up to my front door. I turned to him without making a move to go inside.

"Thank you for driving me home," I said.

Marek reached out and tucked a strand of hair behind my ear.

I suddenly didn't register the cool air around me as every inch of my body heated in response to his touch. I didn't think I'd ever get used to the feel of his skin on mine.

"Stay safe, Ryn. Okay?" Marek whispered.

"I'll try," I told him with a smile.

"You better."

Marek bent and pressed a chaste kiss to my lips. His lips were there and gone so fast that I hardly had a moment to enjoy them. Far too soon, he turned and headed back toward his bike.

I wanted to call out and tell him to wait, to rush down the sidewalk and jump into his arms and kiss him with the passion that raged through my veins. But then his bike roared to life, and he was gone.

My heart flipped in my chest as I watched him disappear. In that moment, it became very clear. No other guy stood a chance. My heart would always belong to the boy who saved my life.

My stomach dropped when I spotted Trenton in the hall the next morning. I still hadn't had a chance to apologize to him. I stared at him for what felt like a full minute, contemplating whether or not to say anything. He looked so sad—almost angry. I couldn't help but blame myself.

"Hey, Trenton," I said softly as I approached him.

Confusions settled on his face when he saw me, like he couldn't understand why I was talking to him.

I leaned against the locker next to his. "Do you have a second?"

"I suppose." He didn't sound very enthused.

I took a deep breath. "I wanted to say I'm sorry. I didn't meant to hurt you. I *do* like you, but… not in that way."

The muscles in Trenton's jaw tightened.

I sighed. "Look, Marek and I had a thing going before you—"

"Before I kissed you?" Trenton snapped. "I don't go around kissing just anyone, Ryn. I actually liked you."

My throat closed up. I hated hurting him like this. Before I could say anything else, Trenton started toward his first class. I instinctively reached out for his wrist. It felt unusually cold.

"We can still be friends, can't we?" I asked.

He dropped his gaze. "I'm not sure if we can. Just… be careful out there, okay?"

"Yeah, I will," I said slowly as he distanced himself from me.

I turned to head to class, but I couldn't get his words out of my mind. Was he trying to *warn* me about something?

"What do you want to practice today?" Marek asked after school in the hall.

Kissing, I thought instantly. The word nearly passed my lips, but I caught myself before it could. God, I was obsessed.

"Fireballs." *Obviously.*

"How many times do I have to tell you—?"

"They're not fireballs," I finished for him. "I know. But doesn't it make it sound cool?"

"They don't even *look* like fireballs," he argued.

"Speak for yourself. Mine are pretty badass." I reached for the basement door and flipped on the light inside the stairwell.

"I'm not going to argue with that," Marek said. "Just don't go throwing any of them at me."

"I won't." I smiled while I descended the steps.

"I think we should see how your essence performs under pressure today. Let's start with a short warm-up."

Marek wrapped his arms around one of the heavy targets and scooted it back against the wall. His shirt rode up. I caught myself admiring his exposed skin, but then I saw something glisten near his waistband. He quickly tugged down on his shirt, and the object disappeared beneath it.

"What?" he asked innocently when he caught me staring.

"Nothing," I lied.

Except, I knew it was *something*. Marek was carrying around the Davina Blade. That meant he was scared of something. Why hadn't he mentioned it?

"Move back," Marek instructed. "Farther... Okay, that's good. Let's see what you've got."

Marek stood next to me out of the line of fire. He was so close that I could feel his body heat and smell the lingering scent of leather on his skin. If this was the pressure he was talking about, it was definitely a distraction.

The target seemed a mile away, but I formed a white ball of essence and drew my arm back. The fireball flew forward and crashed into the middle of the foam target. It exploded with a pop.

"Good," Marek said. "Now, step back farther and try it with your left hand."

Marek had me go through every possible scenario he

could think of. I shot essence over my shoulder, from the ground, and with both hands at once. He even made me race across the basement while I took shots at the target in rapid succession. Over the next hour, my essence never once flickered between white and purple. I considered it a victory.

"I think I need a break." I sank onto the steps because they were the only place to sit.

"Do you think you're going to get a break during a real fight?"

I glared up at him. "Did you notice how many times I hit the target? Any demon would be dead by now whether I conjured the Power of Grace or not."

"And what if it's an army of demons?" Marek challenged, sitting beside me.

An image of Dorian flashed through my mind. I pictured the demons he'd brought with him to the valley to distract my friends with. If Dorian would've let them have their shot at me, I'd have been stunned within seconds and killed in under a minute. I definitely understood where Marek was coming from.

"I'll have you there to protect me," I teased to lighten the mood.

"That's my goal," he said.

I couldn't help but smile. "How'd I get so lucky?"

Marek leaned into me. His soft breath rushed across my face, heating the surface of my skin.

"I'm the lucky one," he whispered.

His gaze dropped to my lips then back to my eyes. He wanted this. I wanted this.

What the hell?

I went for it.

A split second later, my fingers were tangled in his hair, and his tongue danced across my bottom lip. His hands found the bare skin on my back where my tank top had ridden up. I couldn't help it when the smallest moan escaped my lips. He silenced it with another kiss. And then another. And another.

I hardly caught a breath between each kiss. Oxygen didn't seem to matter in the moment. All that mattered was his lips, his hands, and the fire that ignited in my chest when he touched me.

I shifted to draw my body closer to his. Marek's warm hands settled on my hips, and he pulled me into him until I was on his lap. His strong, comforting arms wrapped gently around my middle. I never felt more like I *belonged* somewhere than I did when I was in Marek's arms. It felt so overwhelmingly *right* that I thought I might cry from the flood of emotions coursing through me.

I wanted more. I wanted to melt into him until we became one. My fingers ran up his shirt and across his bare back, and his did the same to mine. It felt as if we'd never get close enough to each other.

Marek pulled away. Good thing he did before we completely lost control. If we made out much longer, my shirt wasn't going to stay on. And once that happened, his pants were fair game.

We both took a moment to catch our breath.

"We should probably get back to practice," he suggested.

My shoulders dropped. "Yeah. Our first mock battle is tomorrow, and I'm so unprepared."

I didn't want this moment to end. I wanted Marek and his lips, his soft skin, his biceps, his—

"You'll do fine," he assured me.

"Not if I don't get a quick bathroom break and a drink," I teased.

And maybe a cold shower.

"Okay," he agreed. "I want to sneak some dodge balls from storage anyway. It'll be a good way to step up the pressure. Go take your water break."

"Thank you." I exaggerated my gratitude and pulled myself up using the railing.

Upstairs, I paused to watch Marek retreat down the hall. I couldn't help it when my eyes locked on his backside. I could picture myself stripping off every layer of clothing he wore.

He rounded the corner, and I snapped back to attention. God, I was a creep. Once he was out of sight, I pushed my way into the girl's restroom.

I stopped at the drinking fountain just outside the door when I'd finished. As I bent over it, movement down the hall caught my eye. Thinking it was Marek, I lifted my head, but no one was there.

Out of nowhere, a black ball flew in my direction. Instinctively, I let out a yelp and ducked out of the way. I quickly rose to my feet again.

So this is Marek's idea of training me to dodge fireballs? Sneaking up on me when I'm not ready for it?

I caught a glimpse of someone's arm at the end of the

hall as they hurled another dark ball my way. This time, I got a good look at it.

A true scream of terror ripped out of my lungs as a glowing black ball of essence sped toward me. I ducked again, but as soon as I lifted my head, another fireball was flying at me. This definitely wasn't a test from Marek.

This was a demon attack.

What the hell was a demon doing in the halls of Galen High?

I took off running. I didn't want to find out the answer to that question. Just as I turned at the end of the hall, a tall figure came out of nowhere and grabbed onto me. I screamed again.

"Shh," Marek demanded.

I quieted instantly. "There—there's someone down the hall… trying to…" I couldn't get the words out.

"Every freaking time I turn my head," he muttered through clenched teeth.

Marek let go of my arms and sprinted down the hall. I hadn't caught up by the time he reached the end of the hall and glanced both ways.

He turned back to me. "There's no one here."

"But there was, Marek! There was!" My voice came out high and shaky.

"I believe you," he said in a breathy voice. "Let's get to Fletcher's classroom. He should still be around."

"Okay," I agreed. My eyes darted around the hall the whole way there.

Fletcher was on the phone when we entered his room in a rush. Alarm settled on his face, and he pulled the phone away from his ear. "Sorry," he said to whoever was on the other end of the line. "I'll call you back."

Marek quickly shut the door behind us.

Fletcher shot up from the chair behind his desk. "What's going on?"

"I—I," I stammered.

"Someone attacked Ryn *again*," Marek said angrily.

"Where?" Fletcher took me by the shoulder and guided me to sit in a nearby desk.

"Here!" Marek's voice rose. "In the school!"

"You can't be serious," Fletcher said in shock.

I managed to find my voice, though my hands continued to shake. "Someone tried to stun me."

Just like they did yesterday.

"Did you see who it was?" Fletcher asked.

"No, but it definitely wasn't a Davina," I said.

Fletcher furrowed his brow.

"It was a demon," I clarified. "Here. At Galen High."

I turned to Marek. "I'm sorry. You were right. This isn't about some stupid drama. Someone's trying to kill me again, but this time they're bolder than Dorian was. I mean… coming into the *school*? They had to be following us, waiting for you to leave me alone."

"You weren't together when this happened?" Fletcher asked with an edge to his tone.

"No," I said. "I was at the drinking fountain when they shot the first fireball at me."

I half expected Marek to tell me they weren't fireballs like he always did.

Instead, he stared forward. "I didn't know what I saw yesterday, but what you're saying confirms it."

"What do you mean?" I asked.

"I couldn't be sure, but yesterday, I thought I saw dark essence hit you right before I saw you fall, but it was out of the corner of my eye. I thought I was being stupid and paranoid. I'm sorry I left you again. The woods right on the edge of town is one thing. I never thought a demon would come into the school."

"What are we going to do?" I asked desperately.

"What happened yesterday?" Fletcher demanded.

Marek quickly explained how I'd been stunned in the forest and apologized for not mentioning it sooner.

"This has only happened when you're alone?" Fletcher asked.

"Yes," I answered.

Fletcher whirled toward Marek and spoke sternly. "I don't want you to let Ryn out of your sight. Not for a moment."

"He'll have to," I said. "He can't exactly stay the night at my house, and we don't have all our classes together."

"Your life is more important," Fletcher insisted. "We'll change Marek's schedule. Allie can stay the night at your house. The way these demons have been working, I don't think you're at risk unless you're alone."

I covered my face in my hands. How much longer did I have to live with being a target for the demons?

"Marek, take Ryn straight home," Fletcher commanded. "I'm going to talk to some people and see if I can't get any news on demon sightings in the area. You're going to be fine, Ryn."

I wasn't sure even he believed his words.

Marek squeezed my hand and led me out of the building to his bike. By the time we reached my house, my fear had turned into anger.

"Are you doing okay?" Marek asked when we reached the porch.

I curled my hands into fists. "I don't know why I ran, Marek. I should've stood my ground and fought."

"You did the right thing coming to find me."

"Next time, I won't," I promised. "I've learned a lot from you in the last few weeks. I think it's time to put that training to the test. Marek, the next time I'm faced with a demon, I'm fighting back."

27

llie stopped by my house that night, and I filled her in on everything that had happened. She didn't seem shocked that I'd been attacked again. It was like it was starting to become a part of my daily routine. Shower, breakfast, school, murder attempt… That was pretty much how my life went these days.

After dinner, I sat on the couch next to Mom. She'd already gotten bored of crocheting and had turned to knitting. At least she was using up the yarn she'd collected.

"What is it?" she asked like she expected me to bring her bad news.

"Allie and I have homework, so she's staying the night."

Mom's lips tightened. "Let me guess. You waited until the last minute?"

I forced a smile. "You know me too well."

Mom sighed. "Don't let this become a regular occurrence."

I left before she could change her mind.

Allie and I hung out in the basement, staring at the Davina carving in the wall. We sat side-by-side on a rug I'd lain across the floor and stressed over every little thing we possibly could.

"I never asked if you found Meg online," I said. "Any chance you got in touch with her?"

Disappointment washed over Allie's face. "No. Sorry. I didn't."

"And Fletcher doesn't know her? If she's a Davina, wouldn't she have gone to Galen High?"

Allie shook her head. "Not if she moved here after high school."

"Good point."

"Are you nervous about tomorrow?" Allie asked.

"What about tomorrow?"

"Our first mock battle."

"You think I'm scared of a little sparring after I've already killed demons? Please. This mock battle is the last thing on my mind."

"Yeah, but it takes place in the woods, in the same place where you've been attacked... how many times is it now?"

"Does it?"

This was the first time anyone mentioned that.

"Tomorrow's battle does," Allie said.

I had to admit, the woods between the school and the valley wasn't exactly my favorite place on the planet, but I wasn't about to let myself get scared over it. I'd been enough of a coward earlier today.

I shrugged. "It's fine. Like I said, I'm ready for anything."

"Are you sure you want to do this?" Fletcher asked the following day during last period. We stood next to the entrance of the trail preparing for our battle. "You don't have to."

"I want to," I assured him. I needed to take my frustrations out somehow. "I'm not going to use essence."

"If you're not going to participate fully—"

"You keep saying I need more training," I pointed out. "Isn't the point of this to put my skills to the test?"

"Yes—" he started.

"Good." I returned to stand by my friends without giving him a chance to respond.

"So, you're going to fight?" Marek asked.

"Yup," I said proudly.

I didn't miss the glance Marek and Fletcher exchanged. The implications of it we're clear: *Don't let her out of your sight*.

"I'll be fine," I assured Marek. "I'm ready for this."

Allie looked uncertain from beside him, but she didn't say anything.

Mrs. Anders blew her whistle, sending my blood pressure skyrocketing. I *hated* that shrill sound.

"Is everyone here?" she called to get our attention.

Our team of five—made complete by one of the sophomore girls, Ruby—stood in a line. Casey's team lined up nearby, opposite us. Unlike other sports I was used to, there weren't any spectators.

"This battle will be a version of capture the flag," Mrs.

Anders explained. "Stunning and sparring are allowed. Once someone has captured your flag, you're out, and you must return here. The boundary is marked by the forest. You may go anywhere between here and the valley, but not beyond. You will see orange stakes marking the other end of the boundary. The last team standing wins. When you hear the whistle, the battle is over. This is a split fight, meaning your team members will be split up before the fight starts. You'll have to find each other if you want to team up. Any questions?"

Nobody responded even though a million questions raced through my mind. Apparently, everyone else had done this enough times to understand the procedure.

"Wouldn't it be easy to cheat?" I whispered to Marek. "Like going beyond the boundaries or stealing your flag back?"

"Refs walk around the arena while we fight," Marek explained.

"Okay," I said. "I think I've got this."

I hadn't realized Mrs. Anders had already started handing out flags to the other team. Each of them secured the flags around their waist so that they poked out in the back like a tail.

I turned to Marek again. "What's up with the flags?"

He whispered softly. "The idea is that if you get close enough to steal someone's flag, you're close enough to kill them."

A shiver ran down my spine at his words.

Mrs. Anders reached our team and handed us each a

flag. I secured mine around my waist. I was ready to take on anything.

My team entered into a huddle.

"What's the plan?" Kyle asked.

Marek quickly took the lead. "We'll meet up at the middle of our boundary line and go from there. Sound good?"

"Yep," Ruby said.

"Saints Rule on one, two, three?" Allie suggested.

Everyone placed their hands into the center of the circle and shouted *Saints Rule* in unison. Before I realized what was happening, our team was following behind a group of referees in blaze orange t-shirts. Casey's team started in the opposite direction. I felt totally lost.

"We start on either end of the arena," Allie said, noticing the confusion on my face.

"How much does this help prepare for a real fight?" I asked.

Marek shrugged. "It can get intense. You'll see."

We entered the forest near one of the orange stakes. I glanced to Marek, then to Allie. They both had looks of determination on their faces, like they were going into a real battle.

Each of us followed a referee to our starting points.

"Good luck," the referee said before walking away and leaving me on my own.

I stood still, listening to the sound of the wind rustling through the trees. The overcast sky blocked the warm sun, and a chill filled the air.

A whistle blew in the distance, signaling the start of the battle. Instead of heading toward the boundary line like Marek had suggested, I turned with determination toward the heart of the forest. I wouldn't always have a team of Davina at my side. This was as good of a time as any to test my skills and prove to myself I could handle a fight on my own.

Marek was going to be *pissed*.

Leaves crunched under my feet, but otherwise, the woods remained silent. I squinted into the trees, and my heart lurched. At the first sign of movement, I threw myself behind a tree for cover.

I listened intently as the person approached. I stole a glance toward the sound and saw blaze orange moving between the trees. It was only one of the refs keeping an eye out for injuries and cheaters. I breathed a sigh of relief and stepped out from behind the tree.

My senses remained on high alert. At one point, I heard a grunt followed by shuffling feet in the distance, indicating that someone had been stunned. I formed a white fireball in my palm when I spotted a girl from Casey's team approaching, but she held her hands up to show that she was already out.

I was quickly starting to get bored.

A stick broke nearby under somebody's weight. My head instantly jerked in the direction of the noise. A white fireball flew toward me, and I ducked instinctively. It hit one of the trees behind me. I stood up straight in a defensive stance.

Casey advanced. "You're all alone, I see."

I formed white essence in my palm, though I didn't

intend to use it. "You, too. You could've stayed with your own team, you know."

Casey stepped around a tree and crinkled her nose. "Nah, it's more fun this way. What's taking you so long? I thought for sure you'd be eager to use your essence now. Don't you want to show me what you've got?"

I swallowed. "I'd rather not hurt you."

"Didn't anyone tell you that's the *point* of this?" she growled.

"I thought the point was to capture the flag."

Casey smiled. "It doesn't hurt to have a little fun doing it."

I gritted my teeth. If Casey wanted a real fight, I'd give her one.

28

I stepped toward Casey, ready for anything she threw at me. Turned out, the first thing she threw was a punch. Pain shot through my cheek bone.

I quickly retaliated. My fist met her jaw with a satisfying *thud*.

That one's for Allie, I thought.

"We're supposed to be sparring, not boxing," I snarled.

"Relax," Casey said, apparently not fazed by the punch. "We both heal fast."

Casey's fist flew out again. Though I made a move to duck, I wasn't quick enough. Her fist hit the side of my head. I barely felt the pain as a fire ignited inside of me. What was this bitch's problem?

Casey kicked her foot out in a swift, controlled motion. I jumped back just in time. We began circling each other.

"What's your problem with me?" Casey asked with a smirk.

I raised an eyebrow. "I could ask you the same question.

It wouldn't happen to have anything to do with my boyfriend, would it?"

Casey's expression faltered momentarily.

It didn't take a genius to realize I'd guessed right. Never mind Marek's preferences or that he had plenty of opportunities to go out with Casey and never took them. None of that mattered in the moment. It was like a silent mutual agreement existed between us that said the last girl standing would win Marek's affection.

I threw another punch in Casey's direction, but she successfully blocked it. It took all I had to keep my fireballs at bay.

"Are we just going to stand here all day?" Casey asked as we continued to circle each other.

I took her question as an invitation and lunged toward her. Her arms instantly came out to block my attack, but it didn't matter. I'd tossed all my weight on top of her, and we tumbled to the forest floor together. She grunted when we landed.

I managed to get in another punch. I was sure she'd end up with a black eye from the blow. An instant later, her hand was in my hair, tugging at the long strands. I cried out in pain and clawed at her face.

"Ow!" she shrieked. "You *bitch*."

"Me?" I asked in disbelief, still trying to struggle away from her grasp. I was a lot of things, but I'd never measure up to Casey's level of bitchiness. It didn't matter that she was a Davina. The girl was evil.

No matter how much I scratched at her face, she didn't loosen her hold on my hair. I did the only thing I could think of and plunged my fingers into her long blond locks. She let out a cry of pain, and her fingers loosened just enough on my hair that I was able to pull back and free myself. I managed to drag a good chunk of her hair with me in my fist.

Casey got to her feet quickly.

I backed up several paces and opened up my hand to let her hair fall to the earth.

"Don't tell me you're scared," she challenged.

"Oh, believe me, I'm only getting started," I threatened.

I threw my body forward again. My knee connected with her ribs. Suddenly, arms and feet were flying faster than I could process them. Casey landed another punch to my jaw and kicked me hard in the thigh. I got a second kick to her ribs and a third to her shin.

Just as another fist swung in my direction, I dodged out of its path. Instead of pulling away from Casey, I spun toward her. My elbow connected with her nose while my other hand reached around her body and plucked the flag from her waist.

Only then did I take several steps back. Casey had fallen to her knees, with both hands pulled protectively to her face. When she withdrew them, I saw that a crimson red liquid coated her palms.

"Whoa. What's going on here?" an unfamiliar voice came through the trees.

Casey and I looked toward the newcomer in surprise. It was one of the refs who was supposed to be observing the arena and making sure this very thing didn't happen. We were only supposed to practice our skills, not hurt each other.

The ref's eyes flickered between the flag in my hand and Casey's bloody face.

Casey held up a hand to stop him. "It's okay. It was an accident."

My jaw nearly dropped. Casey wasn't trying to protect me, was she? Or maybe she was protecting herself, considering she started the fight.

Casey stood, holding onto her bleeding nose. "Ryn won fair and square."

The ref frowned. He didn't believe us.

Casey wiped the blood from her face. "I have to hand it to you, Ryn. You fight better than I thought you would. Just don't think you'll get lucky every time."

Then she turned to head out of the trees.

I could hardly believe my ears. Had Casey *complimented* me? It almost sounded that way, but there was more to it. There'd been a threat in her tone that told me she expected to—or at least wanted to—fight again.

"You two behave yourselves," the ref warned before he headed off to find other fights to observe.

I shoved the flag I'd taken from Casey in my pocket and smiled as she disappeared through the trees. Still high on adrenaline, I started forward quickly in search of another fight.

I stopped abruptly when I saw Marek standing just yards away with his arms crossed over his chest. He did *not* look happy.

"What?" I asked innocently.

"Well, I have some ideas on where you need improvement."

How long had he been watching?

"Improvement?" I asked. "But I won."

Marek looked like he was trying not to roll his eyes. "You won a catfight."

"A catfight?" Truth be told, I couldn't exactly deny that's what it had been. "Okay, maybe I won a catfight, but only thanks to what you've taught me."

Marek raised his eyebrows. "And we have a long way to go."

I shrugged. "I'll get there."

Marek frowned. "You weren't supposed to run off."

"You ran off, too!" I accused. "Where's everyone else?"

"They teamed up like we planned. I came to find you. Should we go find the rest of Casey's team?"

"Fine."

A moment later, another sound reached my ears.

Marek placed himself in front of me. "Let me take this one."

I had to peek around his muscular form to see what was going on. Troy was closing in on us—and quickly.

Marek pushed me. "Run."

I followed his instructions and sprinted away from the oncoming attack. I was starting to see the fun in these mock battles.

I slowed and then turned, expecting Marek to be right behind me, but he was gone.

"Damn it, Marek," I muttered under my breath.

I remained on high alert. I began back the way I came,

hoping to join up with Marek. If I was lucky, I could sneak up on Troy from behind and get a little sparring in before I stole his flag.

I didn't make it very far before movement caught my eye from straight ahead. I didn't have time to process the object coming at me. I threw my body to the earth not a moment too soon. Dark essence whizzed by my head.

Reality hit me a split second later. This was no longer a mock battle.

It was the real thing.

29

*J*umped to my feet and stretched my palm out. I could already feel the white electricity pulsing through my arm. I scanned the trees for movement. My eyes met nothing but bare tree trunks and undergrowth.

"Show yourself!" I demanded.

The air grew still while I waited, but my heartbeat pulsed loudly in my ears. This was nothing like when Casey and I fought. Casey wanted to hurt me, but she didn't want to kill me. A demon wasn't about to offer me the same courtesy.

"I said show yourself!" I yelled.

Another dark fireball sped toward me. As I threw my body behind a nearby tree, I caught sight of motion out of the corner of my eye. The attacker sought cover behind one of the largest trees in the forest.

"What kind of demon are you if you can't face your opponent?" I shouted.

"I'm the kind you don't want to mess with!" he called back.

My breath hitched. I knew that voice, but it definitely didn't belong to a demon.

I didn't have a chance to ask for an explanation before a tall, shirtless figure stepped out from behind the tree. White wings rose out of his back. Though he looked entirely Davina, there was no mistaking that something was amiss. In his right hand glowed white essence, indicating his Davina blood. In his left hovered a black ball of essence I'd only seen demons conjure.

Agony filled my chest at the betrayal.

"What do you think you're doing, Trenton?" I demanded.

"I'm stopping you," he said before he hurled two balls of essence at my head, one light and one dark.

I spun behind the tree again for protection. A moment later, I threw my own white fireball toward him. I knew I told Fletcher I wouldn't use my essence during this fight, but I didn't have a choice but to defend myself.

I just need to stun him, not kill him.

"Stopping me from what?" I yelled from where I crouched for cover.

A twig snapped in the distance under Trenton's weight.

"I know what you're up to." He said it like it was a threat. "I know what you are."

My entire body tensed. How could he possibly know? And why would another Davina want to stop me from awakening Grace?

I need answers.

I sprang up to throw essence toward him again, but I acted too quickly and missed him entirely. He was on the move and closing in on me fast. I hurled another fireball toward him, this time with better aim, but I didn't stick around to see where it landed.

I took off, dodging around trees and jumping over fallen branches to put distance between us. I hardly noticed that I'd passed the boundary marker. Another black orb flew by my head as I ran. I quickly ducked behind another thick trunk.

"We can talk this out, Trenton!" I called. "I thought we were friends."

"We could've been. But not anymore." He stalked toward me with a hard expression on his face. He definitely looked like he was out for blood.

"Maybe tell me why you want me dead," I suggested. "I thought you were going to become a Protector after graduation. You know what it means to protect, don't you?"

Trenton was closing in on me fast. I took my chances and sprinted away.

In the distance, the sound of twigs breaking reached my ears, but it came from a different direction than where Trenton stood. Something in the sound of those footsteps filled me with a sense of hope.

Marek.

He didn't know this mock fight had turned into a real one. I thought about calling out to him, but I realized the moment I opened my mouth that calling him over could get him stunned—or killed.

I have to take Trenton out first.

I stopped behind a large tree for cover. Trenton paused for a moment and looked out toward the sound of approaching feet.

The distraction was a blessing. I hurled three white fireballs toward him in quick succession. The first flew by his ear and pulled his attention back to me just in time for the second to hit his shoulder and the third to hit his chest.

Trenton's tall, muscular body crumbled to the ground. I hurried over to him and fell to my knees. Marek arrived a second later.

He gazed down at Trenton in confusion. "I thought you weren't going to stun anyone."

"I wasn't," I said flatly. "Marek, it was Trenton."

His brows came together. "What do you mean?"

"I think it's safe to assume he's the one who's been trying to kill me."

"What are you talking about? Trenton's a Davina."

I looked down at Trenton's face and shook my head. "I'm not sure he's entirely Davina."

Marek crouched to my level. "Ryn, what are you talking about?"

"Doesn't matter," I said.

I whirled to my right and then my left in search of anything that might immobilize Trenton before he woke. My gaze fell upon my shoes. I instantly began untying my laces.

"We have to get him to talk. Here, help me." I wrenched the shoelace from my tennis shoe and held it out to Marek before turning to the second one.

Marek took the lace but didn't make a move.

"Marek, I'm serious. Trenton can conjure dark essence. He said he wanted to stop me. He said he knew what I was up to."

"You don't think he was talking about Grace, do you?"

"I do."

"Why would he want to stop you?"

"My question exactly. Now hurry up!"

Marek seemed to catch the urgency in my tone. He rounded Trenton's unmoving body and hoisted him into a seated position against a nearby tree. Marek began securing one of my laces around Trenton's left wrist. I did the same to the right.

Trenton made a small noise, indicating that he was waking up. Marek tugged at the laces to confirm they were secure. I wasn't sure they'd hold, but they were the best thing we had.

"Give it to me," I demanded, stretching my palm out toward Marek.

"Give you what?"

"The Davina Blade. I know you have it."

Marek took a step back. "What makes you think I have it?"

"You're wasting time," I snapped. "You've been carrying it around. I know it."

Marek sighed and reached into the back of his jeans. "Be careful with it."

"Thank you," I said as I snatched the weapon from his hands.

I crouched next to Trenton and pressed the blade to his throat. At the cool touch of metal, he inhaled a deep breath.

I thought for a moment I read fear in his expression, but it quickly turned to anger when he realized what was happening.

"Holy shit!" Trenton cried.

"Yeah, that's a knife against your throat," I assured him. "Unless you want to see what it's capable of, you'll answer my questions. What are you?"

"I'm a Davina," he answered quickly.

I pressed the blade tighter against his skin. "Do *not* test me. I've killed demons before. I'm not afraid to kill you if I have to. Let me ask this again. What *are* you?"

"Ryn," Marek whispered. He placed a hand on my shoulder like he thought I was being too hard on Trenton.

I shrugged him off.

"Fine," Trenton said through gritted teeth. "I'm half Aedes."

Marek shifted beside me. I probably wouldn't have believed it either if I hadn't witnessed it myself.

"How do you know what I am?" I asked harshly.

Trenton didn't answer at first. He only stared back at me.

I applied more pressure to the blade. "How do you know?"

Trenton pressed the back of his head against the tree to relieve as much pressure as he could on his neck. "I saw it!"

"When?" I demanded.

This was exactly what Fletcher had been talking about. He didn't want us to tell anyone about my power because he didn't want the wrong person finding out. I thought we'd been careful. I was terribly mistaken.

"When you were fighting those Aedes in the valley before school started," Trenton admitted. "Casey, Troy, and I were there earlier that night. Not long after we left, I saw the light coming from the valley. I ditched Casey and Troy and came back to check it out. I saw you fighting the Aedes. I was going to join in, but I didn't..."

"Didn't what?" I demanded.

Trenton gritted his teeth. "I didn't know which side to fight on! It's one thing to talk about killing the Aedes. It's another to see it in person. Then you conjured purple essence. I'd heard the stories. I knew what it meant."

"Then what happened?" I asked.

"Are you *trying* to kill me?" he snapped.

I realized I'd drawn a small amount of blood. I glanced at it for a second to see that it was a darker shade of red than it should've been. Trenton might've had white Davina wings, but he definitely had demon blood running through his veins.

I pulled back slightly, but not enough to make him think he was safe. "What. Happened. Next?"

"I was supposed to follow you for information," Trenton said.

"That's why you tried to befriend me," I accused.

My heart broke at the thought. My instinct had failed me with Trenton. I should've at least listened to Allie.

"You *were* stalking me!" I realized. "You were always trying to get me to tell you what I was up to, always trying to coerce a bit of information out of me. You even tried to get me to admit I was different!"

I recalled the day we flew together and how he'd asked

me about my talents. The whole time, he'd been trying to get me to tell him about Grace. I couldn't believe I thought he was just being nice.

"I actually believed you liked me," I said in disgust. How could I have been so gullible?

"I did like you," Trenton admitted. "I almost backed out of the whole plan for you."

"What exactly *was* your plan?" I narrowed my eyes.

"I knew you were searching for Grace," Trenton said. "I was supposed to let you lead me to her."

"*You're* the one who overheard Allie and me talking about her." It wasn't a question.

I thought back to Monday afternoon and the conversation Allie and I had outside the jewelry shop. I wondered how much we'd given away, how much Trenton had heard.

"Yeah, I overheard you," he snapped. "Once I knew where Grace was, they said I could take you out. Once you were gone, there was no chance of awakening her. And if we knew where she was, we could destroy her, too."

"Who's 'they?'" Marek asked from beside me.

Trenton closed his eyes like he was in agony. "The Aedes."

"Which ones? Is there a group of them?" Marek's voice became harsh.

"There will be," he admitted with a grimace.

"What do you mean?" I asked. "Someone's building an army? Who?"

Trenton didn't answer.

I dug the blade deeper into his skin. "Who?"

Trenton burst. "My father!"

30

The forest went silent. Trenton's words echoed in my mind.

"Start from the beginning," I told him sternly. "How do you go from being good one moment to evil the next? Tell us *everything*."

Trenton's eyes remained closed, like he was truly scared I might slit his throat. "Fine, but you're in for a long story."

I leaned in closer. "I have time."

Trenton looked so pale I thought he might puke. "The first thing you should know is that my mom was a Davina, and my dad was Aedes. If you think my dad was the evil one just because my mom was an angel, you're wrong. She abandoned me the second she gave birth. I needed food and shelter, but my dad couldn't provide any of that. So I got dropped off at my Davina grandmother's house. She, of course, knew what I was. She let my dad hang around. Despite being Aedes, he still cared. Oh, don't look so surprised."

Trenton narrowed his eyes at Marek before turning his gaze back to me. "My grandma died when I was fifteen. I had no choice but to turn to my mom's brother. I met him a couple of times, and he knew what I was. But he was ashamed."

By the tone of his voice, it was clear he had some pent up anger he needed to get out.

"That's what brought me to Eagle Valley. My father wasn't welcome here. If he even tried to step into town, he'd be killed on the spot. So there I was, completely unwanted in a town of people who would kill me if they knew my secret."

"They wouldn't have killed you," Marek argued.

Trenton's brows shot up. "Sure about that? Who's the one with the knife to his throat?"

"I wouldn't have to if you weren't trying to kill me," I said. "Finish your story."

Trenton breathed heavily. "I had to play along and pretend I was completely Davina even though I'd grown up being both. Turns out Galen High wasn't as bad as I thought it'd be. I mean, at least the hottest girl in town was willing to fool around with me. Couldn't be too bad, could it?"

He had to be talking about Casey. The thought made me want to hurl.

"She changed my mind about things. I started to think that maybe this was where I actually belonged. I *wanted* to become a Protector. I convinced myself my Aedes side meant nothing, that my father was just an anomaly."

"Changed your mind pretty quickly, didn't you?" I snarled.

"When I saw you fighting those Aedes, it was like…"

"Like *what*?" I demanded.

Trenton's words poured out of him quickly. "It was like watching you kill my father!"

He took a deep breath before continuing at a normal pace. "I realized then that I'd lived in Eagle Valley so long without Aedes that I forgot what it was like for one of them to actually *care* about me. My uncle sure as hell didn't. Casey only cared when it worked in her favor."

Did he have to put that image in my mind *again*?

"Then what?" I asked. "You just decided that because no one cared, it was a good idea to kill me?"

The anger in Trenton's eyes intensified. "No. I left town for a couple of days to find my father."

"And?" I asked.

"And I already told you the rest! I told him about you, and he told me to come back and find out where Grace was. I was supposed to prevent you from awakening her and then wait for him. I've done a pretty good job so far, haven't I?"

I ignored his question. "So he's building an army?"

"Yes," Trenton said. "I already told you. He can't exactly stroll into Eagle Valley on his own. He's going to be coming with all the Aedes he can round up."

Marek scoffed from beside me.

"What?" I asked him without tearing my gaze from Trenton.

"Demons aren't exactly a community race," Marek

explained. "How many will he be able to round up? A dozen?"

More than that. I instantly thought of Dorian and the six other demons he managed to round up in a day.

"No, they're not," Trenton agreed. "But that's only because they've never had anything to come together for before. Now they actually have something to fight for."

"Why would you want to fight with them?" I asked.

"Because—ow—would you get that thing off my neck?"

"No," I snapped.

"Because the Aedes deserve this world as much as the Davina do," Trenton answered.

"What about the humans?" Marek said with an edge to his tone. "An influx of demons will destroy the humans more than your race already has."

Trenton scoffed. "I won't even try to explain it to you. You'd never believe the truth anyway."

I gritted my teeth. "Tell us—"

"What's going on here?" a stern voice called.

I tore my gaze from Trenton's face to find Fletcher walking toward us. We'd been so engaged in conversation that none of us noticed his approach.

"This isn't a real battle!" Fletcher exclaimed.

Marek stepped forward. "It's more real than you might believe."

Fletcher's eyes darted between mine and Marek's. "What are you talking about?"

I glared at Trenton. "It's been him all along. He overheard us talking about the key outside of Angela's. He's been trying to kill me ever since."

"That's absurd," Fletcher said.

"He's half demon," I stated flatly like that would explain it all.

Fletcher opened his mouth, but I was already speaking to Trenton before he could say anything.

"You didn't get the key, though, did you? You never heard where it actually was."

"Didn't matter," he said like it amused him. "At first, I was going to get the key so that you couldn't. When I didn't find it, I figured it was better to kill you before you could get to it first. I didn't need you after I overheard where Grace was."

He smiled like he was proud of himself.

It took all my strength not to dig the blade deeper into his throat. "You didn't do a very good job of that, did you?"

"I hadn't planned on anyone finding out it was me! Marek kept showing up and getting in the way."

"Yeah, he has a thing for saving my life," I said before turning to Fletcher. "What do we do with him?"

"He's a demon," Marek said in a harsh tone. He didn't have to say the rest for me to understand what he meant.

He's a demon, and it's our job to kill demons.

"It doesn't matter what you do to me," Trenton cut in. "My father will be here soon."

Marek and Fletcher exchanged a glance. I made the mistake of turning my eyes away from Trenton to watch their exchange.

Trenton's body moved quickly, faster than I could process it. My heart leapt into my throat as his hand snapped to my wrist and squeezed tightly. In a swift motion, he spun me around and pinned me to his chest. His hand gripped my fingers so that I couldn't drop the blade.

I was surprised by my strength as I struggled against his attempt to bring the blade to my throat. In a split second, I managed to wiggle my other arm free of his and swing my elbow back into his face. He loosened his grip just enough that I was able to dig my heels into the ground and distance myself from him.

Marek and Fletcher acted quickly. Two white fireballs sped toward Trenton. He dove to the side just in time for both fireballs to explode against the tree we'd tied him to.

Trenton sprang to his feet and spread his white wings. He launch himself upward and disappeared above the canopy before anyone had a chance to stun him.

"Shit," Marek said. "I knew those laces weren't going to hold."

"Of course they weren't," I snapped. "They were just to hold him there for a bit. The Davina Blade did the rest."

"The blade didn't kill him," Marek replied.

"He was a student!" Fletcher sounded horrified.

"He's a demon!" Marek roared. "He tried to kill Ryn. He's probably flying off to tell the demons everything he knows."

Fletcher breathed heavily. "We have to wake Grace now. No matter what it takes to get to her."

I handed Marek the blade, and he slipped it into the sheath hidden beneath his waistband.

Fletcher led us out of the forest near the trailhead. Casey looked at us smugly, clearly thinking we'd both lost our flags. Three of her teammates lined up beside her. On our team, Kyle and Ruby had returned flagless, which meant Allie was still out there in the trees somewhere.

"What's going on?" Mrs. Anders asked. "Did I just see a student fly out of the trees?"

Fletcher frowned, clearly no longer interested in this game. "Trenton forfeit, but we have bigger problems."

"He just left?" Mrs. Anders asked.

"Yes," Fletcher confirmed. "Call everyone back, please."

Mrs. Anders raised her eyebrows like she couldn't believe a student would just leave in the middle of a battle. She brought her whistle to her mouth to call Allie and the referees back.

"Wait!" Casey cried. "This isn't fair. If a member of our team dropped out, that means they had an advantage."

I didn't bother pointing out that three of our teammates remained standing. It didn't matter.

"We'll get a rematch, won't we?" Casey demanded.

I couldn't hold myself back. "Is that all that matters to you?"

"*What?*" Casey bit back like she couldn't believe I was speaking to her.

"You *have* to win every time, don't you?" I strode toward her swiftly until she was only an arm's length away.

"I'd be careful if I were you," Casey warned. "We had plenty of time for this during the mock battle, and—"

"Life isn't a mock battle!" I yelled.

I was vaguely aware of Marek and Fletcher insisting I calm down, but I ignored them.

"We're Davina," I stated. "We're fighting a real war. When you get out there in the real world, you're not going to be keeping score with *flags.*"

I ripped my flag from my waist and threw it at her feet

to make a point. My breath became shallow as anger coursed through my body.

"You're going to be keeping score by how many people you lose!"

Casey blinked a few times, shocked by my outburst.

I lowered my voice to a normal level. "Trenton left. By my count, you've already lost one person."

Casey didn't say anything as I headed back to my team. Allie had made it out of the woods and saw my exchange with Casey.

"We need to go," I insisted when I made it back to my team.

I didn't know how much time we had left before Trenton's father arrived with his army of demons. *Soon* could mean anything between a few hours to several weeks. I didn't like the uncertainty.

"What's going on?" Mrs. Anders asked.

Fletcher turned to her. "There's no time to explain."

He gestured for our team to follow him. Even though Mrs. Anders shouted questions in Fletcher's direction, he ignored her.

"Mr. Fletcher," Ruby said, sounding confused, "what's going on?"

"I'm sorry, Ruby," he said without looking at her, "but this doesn't concern you. Go home and get some rest. I'll try to explain when this is all over."

She's too young for this, I thought. *He's trying to protect her.*

Ruby drew her eyebrows together. She hesitated momentarily, but she agreed. Ruby left before we made it back to Fletcher's classroom.

Fletcher paced back and forth in front of the white-board, thinking.

"Will someone please tell me what's going on?" Allie blurted.

"Yeah," Kyle agreed.

I opened my mouth to explain, but Fletcher cut in before I could.

"We've run out of time. I thought we had more."

"We've never had time!" I blurted before I could stop myself.

Fletcher's eyes locked on me. It was clear what I was saying; there were things he still didn't know.

"No more secrets, Fletcher. I've had the Power of Grace for a long time," I explained quickly. "The first time I used it, I was eight. That must mean the portal has been a threat longer than you thought."

Fletcher's brows constricted.

I turned to Allie and Kyle. "Fletcher was right. We can't trust all Davina. Trenton found out, and now there's an army of demons on their way into town. They want to stop us from awakening Grace."

Allie's jaw dropped, and Kyle's eyes widened.

"Trenton has something to do with that?" Kyle asked.

"He has everything to do with it," I said.

"But why would—" Allie started.

Marek quickly cut in. "Trenton's half demon."

He proceeded to give them a condensed version of what we'd discovered in the woods.

While he spoke, my phone began vibrating.

"Shit," I muttered under my breath. I didn't have time for a phone call.

I slipped the phone out of my pocket. I didn't recognize the number, but instinct told me to answer.

I pulled the phone to my ear. "Hello?"

"Um, hi," a woman's voice came over the line. "This is Meg."

"Meg!" I exclaimed in excitement.

Everyone stopped to look at me.

"Yeah, I'm calling to let you know I got your message."

"I know what your key goes to," I told her. "Would you be interested in testing it out?"

"How do you know what it opens?" She sounded genuinely curious.

"I found a carving that matches the design," I explained.

"You said it has something to do with the Davina?"

"Yes. If we meet up, I can explain everything."

"Um… okay. Where do you want to meet?"

"My house."

"Where do you live?" She didn't sound like she was committed to the idea yet.

I gave her the address.

"You're kidding," she said in shock.

"No."

"That was my grandpa's house! We sold it after he died."

"So, can you meet me there?" I asked.

"What time works for you?"

"Right now," I answered eagerly.

"Okay. Give me a couple of minutes and I'll be on my way."

I hung up.

"Okay. Let's go," Fletcher said with determination.

"No," I said sternly.

Eyes widened around me. Everyone seemed shocked that I'd speak to Fletcher that way.

I was the one who'd been touched by Grace. It was time I started taking that role seriously. I was in charge now.

"We're done with the secrets," I said. "You can't protect me anymore. You need to round up as many Davina as you can and tell them what's going on. Eagle Valley needs to be prepared for an attack."

Fletcher relaxed and rose his head proudly. "I'll do my best."

"Good." I turned to my friends. "As for the rest of you, it's time to wake Grace."

I burst through front door of my house minutes later. My friends followed closely behind. I quickly kicked off my loose shoes at the door and slipped on my mom's since we were the same size.

"Kathryn?" Mom called from the living room.

"Sorry, Mom," I said in a rush. "Don't really have time. Ancient Davina in the basement that needs awakening and all that."

Mom called my name again just as my hand hit the doorknob to the basement. She stepped into the hall. "What's going on?"

"Sorry, Mom. Totally forgot to tell you that a demon tried to kill me a few weeks ago. Now an army is on their way to try to do it again. We need to get to Grace as soon as we can."

A horrified expression crossed her face. "And you think I'm just going to let you walk head-first into danger?"

"Try to stop me," I challenged.

Mom's eyes glistened at the threat of tears.

"Everything will be fine once I wake Grace," I assured her. "You have nothing to worry about. The demons can't touch you."

"But they can touch *you*." Mom sounded scared. "I thought you didn't know how to get to Grace."

"We know the person who has the key. Speaking of which…" I hurried into the living room and looked out the window. "Where is she? She should be here by now."

"Let's just cool down and be patient," Kyle said.

I whirled toward him. "We don't have time for patience! We've run out of time!"

Marek placed his hands on my shoulders to calm me, but I shrugged him off.

"Come on, Meg…" I pulled my phone from my pocket and punched my fingers at the screen.

How long will you be? I texted.

Several agonizing minutes passed without her response. I paced around the living room, unable to sit still. Finally, I heard the sound of an approaching vehicle and stole another glance out the window. A blue sedan pulled up to the curb. I raced to the front door and opened it before Meg was even on the porch.

"Hi," I greeted her quickly.

Meg stepped inside and glanced around. "I have so many memories here. It looks so different, but some things will always be the same, like the stained glass window." She turned to my mom and smiled. "Hi, I'm Margaret."

"Oh," Allie said, dragging out the word. "I thought Meg was short for Megan."

"Nope," Meg said. "Margaret, like my grandma."

That explained why Allie couldn't find her online. She'd been searching the wrong name.

"Yeah, that's great and all, but we—"

The sound of Marek's ringtone cut me off.

"It's Fletcher." Marek answered immediately and put him on speakerphone.

"Is it done?" Fletcher's voice came over the line.

"Not yet," I said desperately.

"Hurry up," Fletcher demanded. "A group of Aedes have been spotted flying just outside of town. We're luring them to the valley. Get there as soon as you can. It's time to fight."

Shit. We really were out of time.

Meg's eyes widened. "The Aedes are *here?*"

"Yes, but we need—"

"My parents will want to fight, but my dad..." Meg's eyes widened in horror. "I'm sorry. I can't let him fight. I have to go."

"Wait, Meg!"

She didn't wait for an explanation. She spun around and sprinted back to her vehicle.

"Stop!" I called, chasing after her. "We need the key to—"

She was already in her vehicle. The engine roared to life.

"The Davina need you here!" I cried.

She never heard me.

"God dammit!" I whirled around to see my friends had followed me outside.

"Shit," Marek muttered through clenched teeth. He stared after Meg's car with an expression of disbelief on his face.

Kyle and Allie exchanged a worried look.

I hesitated for only a moment. "Screw this. We're going to help."

"Wait!" Marek stopped me. "You shouldn't go. We need you to stay safe. If you get hurt—"

"You think you're going to be able to keep me away?" I challenged.

Marek's shoulders dropped in defeat. He knew he couldn't.

I started across the lawn toward Allie's car. Everyone followed, including my mother.

I stopped abruptly. "You're not coming, Mom."

"Like hell I'm not!" she argued.

"You can't even see the demons!"

"We've already been through this," she said sternly. "I may not be able to see them, but they can't touch me."

"Not unless they get their hands on our Davina Blade. That thing exists across all planes and could hurt any of us." It was a long shot, but it was the only argument I could come up with.

"Don't worry," Kyle said as Marek handed him the blade. "I'm not letting any demons get their hands on it."

I reached out and pulled my mom into a hug. "You're not going to stop me from doing this. Please stay here and be safe."

Mom stared after me speechlessly as my friends and I climbed hastily into Allie's car.

Allie fumbled with the keys for a moment and then whipped out of the driveway.

"I love you!" my mom called after me.

Allie put the car into gear and tore off down the street, blowing through the stop sign at the end of our block.

Tires squealed as she slammed on the brakes in front of Galen High.

I kicked the car door open and raced across the grass. My breath caught in my chest as my eyes turned to the sky. A dense black cloud of smoke rose above where the valley hid in the forest. It was in motion but didn't follow any particular pattern. I slowed momentarily.

"Oh my God." Marek stopped beside me.

The trees weren't on fire. It wasn't a black cloud of smoke.

It was a flock of winged demons.

"I hope Fletcher rounded up enough reinforcements," Kyle said under his breath.

I took off running again. Before I made it to the trees, I flexed my wings and launched myself into the gray sky. I was aware of three other sets of wings flapping behind me. I dove straight into the middle of the fight, aiming white essence at demon after demon. Black wings flapped all around me. Occasionally, white wings appeared.

Once I was directly above the valley, I was finally able to take in the sheer number of people fighting. Black cloaks dominated up here in the sky, but white wings were most prevalent on the ground. Some Davina fought hand-to-hand while others stunned demons out of the air. The entire town must've been here—at least, the Davina portion of it. There had to be hundreds of us. But we were still outnumbered.

Dark essence flew by my head, pulling my attention from the ground and back to the sky. I turned to face my attacker, but there were so many bodies flying through the air that it was impossible to tell who it'd come from. I threw several more fireballs toward the demons closest to me and then dove to join the Davina on the ground.

Marek landed beside me and shot essence into the air. It hit a demon in the head. He spiraled out of the sky and landed a few yards from us. A sickening *crunch* met my ears as the demon's neck broke upon impact. He disappeared in a puff of black smoke, leaving behind nothing but his cloak.

I shot a white fireball at an approaching demon. More and more demons landed in the grass to fill the valley. Nearby, I noticed a young girl with red hair taking on two demons at once. Fletcher told her to go home only half an hour ago. It seemed like an entire lifetime since our mock battle ended.

Ruby kicked one of the demons in the gut and then spun and threw a white fireball at the other. He collapsed, stunned. She made the mistake of taking a split second to relish in her victory before the other demon caught her and wrapped a strong arm around her throat. Somehow, through the deafening sound of shouts and flapping wings, I could hear her gasping for air.

I didn't take a moment to think about it. I formed white essence in my palm and aimed it at the demon's face. It hit him square on, and he crumbled to the ground.

Ruby was momentarily confused, like she couldn't figure out where the demon had gone. Then her eyes fell on me.

"What the hell are you doing here?" I demanded as I abandoned Marek and raced over to her. I shot another fireball at the demon running up behind her. "I thought Fletcher told you to go home."

Ruby held her head up proudly. "Yeah, and then I came back. I heard you needed all the help you can get."

"But you're only fifteen!" I grabbed onto her shoulders, and we ducked another attack. The dark essence fizzled out behind us.

"So what?" Ruby asked. "Fletcher thought I was good enough to fight with you earlier."

"That was a stupid exercise! It's nothing compared to this. You could die out here!"

Another white fireball left my palm when I spotted a demon too close for comfort.

"So could you," Ruby said stubbornly. "Besides, I've been training longer than you have."

It was clear there was nothing I could say to convince her to leave.

"Don't let your guard down," I instructed.

"I won't," she assured me before sending a fireball toward a demon behind me.

I left her on her own and sprinted through the crowd, knocking out as many demons as I could along the way. Nearby, I spotted Kyle with his blade.

"Kyle, duck!" I shouted just in time for him to barely miss being stunned.

Allie fought beside him, working with him as if they were a single unit. She reached out for the blade just as another demon swooped down out of the sky. She spun and sliced the blade across the demon's throat. Blood spurted, and a line of deep red liquid covered Allie's white wings. It didn't even slow her down.

I stopped in my tracks. The sound of battle faded around me as I spun to take in the scene.

Troy tackled a demon to the ground, but a second demon jumped on top of him a moment later. He took Troy's wing in his hands and wrenched on it. Troy cried out in pain. Casey shot a fireball at the demon, and he fell to the ground. Troy's wing hung at an odd angle, the bones in it broken.

A man who looked strikingly similar to Casey fought beside her. I watched in shock as his hands clamped around a demon's head. He twisted. I didn't hear the crack, but I saw the demon go limp and vanish a second later.

This entire battle was a blood bath.

All of this happened in mere seconds, but it was enough to momentarily distract me. I just barely caught sight of a demon flying toward me from out of the corner of my eye.

The demon landed and faced me. His hood had fallen, displaying his skeleton-like features and black irises. In one swift motion, I swung my leg out and knocked him off his feet. Marek rushed over to me and threw himself on top of the demon before I had a chance to blink. Marek's strong fist crashed into the demon's trachea. The demon gasped for breath.

Marek didn't wait around to watch him die. He sprang

to his feet and took my hand. We only made it a few more feet before another black fireball flew by my head.

When I glanced toward the source, my eyes didn't meet the sight of a hooded figure as I expected. Instead, a shirtless man with white wings stalked toward me.

Apparently I hadn't scared him off earlier. Trenton still wanted me dead.

Trenton drew his arm back again, and I kicked myself into the air. His essence exploded where I'd just been standing. I flew up into the swarm of demons, hoping to lose him. When I glanced back, I saw he was closing in on me. I quickly shot a white fireball at him, but he dodged it. It disappeared into the crowd.

Marek found his way between me and Trenton, using his own body as a shield to protect me.

I wove between bodies, flying upward then diving down, dodging wings from left to right. Marek stayed close behind me. No matter how hard we tried to disappear into the crowd, Trenton kept up with us.

I didn't know how this was going to end, but I knew it wasn't going to end up here. Flapping my wings as hard as I could, I dove toward the upper edge of the valley. My feet landed hard in the grass. I ignored the pain and grabbed Marek's hand when he landed beside me. We raced into the trees. I skidded to a halt behind a thick stump and pulled my wings into me, breathing heavily. Marek took cover behind the tree beside me.

"What are you screwing around for?" he hissed. "Use the Power of Grace!"

I didn't answer.

In the thickness of the forest, the sound of flapping wings and screams grew quiet. I could almost pretend nothing was happening past the edge of the trees.

I sensed Trenton land nearby.

"That was quick," I shouted toward him. "Didn't take you long to find your dad and call him into town, did it?"

"He was already on his way." Trenton's voice grew closer and closer as he spoke. "Told you he'd bring an army."

"You don't even understand what you're fighting for!" I accused. "Demons don't even fully exist here."

I flinched when the tree I leaned against shook as Trenton threw another fireball toward me.

"I'm sick of listening to you talk," Trenton sneered. "Why don't you come out and face me?"

"I don't want to kill you," I said truthfully.

Marek shot me a look. *He's a demon.*

But he's a Davina, too, I wanted to argue.

Trenton laughed. I could tell by the sound of his voice that he was only ten yards away.

"You think I'm scared of you?" he asked.

"You should be." It wasn't a threat. It was simple fact.

A white fireball was ready in my hands. I leapt out from behind my tree, but before I could aim at the tall, muscular figure before me, Marek sprang forward and knocked

Trenton to the ground. Trenton rolled away from him and quickly got to his feet.

"Leave her the hell alone!" Marek shouted.

"Screw you!" Trenton roared.

"Marek! Trenton!" I yelled.

Marek had already tackled Trenton to the ground again. Trenton tried to get back up, but Marek threw another kick. Trenton was back on the ground in under a second. Marek swung his foot at Trenton's face over and over again.

All I could do was watch in horror. I didn't want to be a part of this, of the fighting, the bloodshed.

Dark blood rushed from Trenton's face, splattering onto leaves beneath him. Without warning, an angry roar burst from Trenton's chest. He rolled just outside of Marek's reach, giving him enough time to jump to his feet. Trenton lunged forward, and his body slammed into Marek's. He pinned Marek against a tree as his strong fingers wrapped around Marek's neck and sought to strangle the life out of him.

Marek's hands clawed at Trenton as he struggled to free himself, but Trenton was just as strong, if not stronger.

"Let him go!" I growled. I threw myself onto Trenton's back. My fingernails scraped across his face repeatedly.

"Get off of me." With one hand still pinning Marek to the tree, he reached behind him with the other. His cold fingers tangled in my hair, and he tugged. Hard.

I landed on my side in the dirt, my skull aching.

Trenton turned back to Marek with fury in his eyes. Marek's face had gone purple from lack of oxygen. He gasped for breath that never came. He flailed, but most of the fight had already drained out of him. He was on the brink of passing out.

"NO!" I screamed.

I scrambled to my feet and wrenched at Trenton's strong arms, but they didn't budge. Trenton swung an arm out. His elbow slammed into my chest and sent me stumbling backward.

As Trenton's fingers tightened around Marek's throat and he gasped for breath, one thing became very clear to me. Trenton had spent a lifetime fighting between his demon and Davina instincts. His demon side had won. He'd find pleasure in watching the life drain from Marek's eyes.

"Trenton," I begged.

Trenton's lips curled back, and his eyes narrowed, filling his expression with rage.

My time for apologies was over. There was no more reasoning with him. I had only one option left to save Marek.

I don't want to do this, I thought.

I had no other choice.

I pressed my eyes shut tightly and lunged at Trenton. My palm slammed into his bare chest as a flash of purple erupted from my hand. Trenton's body flew backward and crashed to the forest floor several yards away. I flinched.

Marek slumped down the tree onto his back. He inhaled deep, audible breaths.

"Marek!" I cried. I fell to my knees beside him and placed my hands on the side of his face.

"I'm okay," he said in a raspy whisper.

Marek's eyes widened. I followed his gaze and shot to my feet. A purple fireball formed in my hand in a split second. A demon stood several yards past Trenton's unmoving form. But he didn't stick around for a fight. He jumped into the air and flew out of the forest through a break in the trees.

I drew my arm back to aim my fireball at him, but I never took the shot. I lowered my hand to my side and dropped to my knees again. I didn't want to fight anymore.

Slowly, I lifted my gaze and turned my attention to Trenton. He lay sprawled out on the ground with his white wings stretched wide. His arms lay limp at his side.

A lump so large rose to my throat that I struggled to breathe. Unlike the demons that disappeared as soon as their life energy could no longer tether them to a stable plane, Trenton's body remained. His lifeless eyes stared up into the canopy above us.

I couldn't bear to see him like that. Slowly, I crawled over to him and gently closed his eyelids. And then I threw my body over his chest and wept.

34

"*R*yn!"

I was vaguely aware of someone calling my name. I didn't know how much time had passed, but when I raised my head to identify the source of the voice, I noticed that dusk had settled over the forest.

Marek sat beside me with a comforting hand rested on my shoulder.

A chill breeze brushed across my arms and sent a shiver down my spine. I sat up to wipe at the tears on my cheeks, but they'd already dried.

"Ryn! Marek! Oh my God." Allie skidded to a halt beside us and dropped to pull me into a hug. "We couldn't find you. We thought that maybe you—you…"

Hot tears rose to my eyes again at the sight of Trenton's body. "I—I killed him, Allie. We were going to die. It was the only way to stop him."

No, I told myself. *I could've stunned him instead. Stunned him and walked away. That's what I should've done. All I* wanted to do was turn back time and take back what I'd done.

Allie squeezed me tighter, and I buried my face in her shoulder. "It's okay, Ryn. You had to."

"Is it over?" I whispered.

"It is for now," Allie said gently. "The demons retreated."

I pulled away from her. "They'll be back with more."

"Yeah," Marek agreed in a quiet voice. "There'll be plenty who want to see that portal open."

"We should get back and let everyone know you two are all right," Allie said.

I dared to steal a final glance at Trenton. In the dimming light, he was only an outline.

"What do we do with him?" I asked.

Allie took a deep breath. "We'll have to bury him with the others."

I thought I might hurl. I didn't have to ask for confirmation. Allie's sorrowful tone said it all.

We'd lost others. A lot of them.

"Come on," Allie encouraged.

I could hardly think straight as we distanced ourselves from Trenton's body. We broke through the trees, giving us a clear view of the valley below us.

Nausea slammed into my gut at the sight. Black cloaks littered the valley as if they were the ghosts of the demons lost today. Dozens of unmoving Davina lay beneath us. Those who were still alive moved slowly and solemnly, taking in the devastation. Stillness settled over the valley as if nature itself mourned our losses.

A pained shriek reached my ears. Somehow, it seemed more appropriate than the silence.

My eyes quickly found the woman who'd screamed. She dropped to her knees beside a man's body and took his hand in hers.

I forced down the lump in my throat and summoned my wings. Marek and Allie followed behind me as I flew down to land in the center of the battlefield. Closer up, I had a better view of everyone's faces.

Tears rolled down my cheeks as I took note of the Davina we'd lost. Some I didn't recognize. Most I did.

The woman who'd screamed knelt above a dark-skinned man with broad shoulders. *Mr. Collins.* Beside him, a woman's neck twisted at an odd angle. *Mrs. Banks.* Mrs. Presley, our principal, lay next to her with her lifeless eyes turned to the sky.

I abandoned Marek and Allie and rushed from body to body, praying the familiar faces would end. They didn't.

I saw Troy, with his white wings mangled beneath him. A long bruise lined his neck where he'd been strangled.

Then I noticed Ruby knelt over another young girl's body. Tears fell down her face and splashed onto the other girl's shirt.

"Emily," I whispered.

The second sophomore girl on our training team had somehow found her way to the fight. And it cost her her life.

Gently, I lowered myself to Ruby's side and wrapped an arm around her. "Ruby, I'm so sorry."

She didn't answer past the tears.

Through the darkness, I could see Marek and Kyle carrying Trenton's body out of the trees and down the stairs. They placed him at the end of the row that'd been started to gather our dead.

Scanning the crowd, I noticed that several people nearby had sustained serious injuries. One guy's arm bent in the wrong direction, and another woman's nose was broken. Two girls from my flying class sat wrapped in each other's arms. One girl's wings were twisted. I wasn't sure she'd ever fly again. Nearby, I spotted Casey and her father arguing in hushed whispers about her decision to join the fight.

And then my eyes fell upon another familiar face. Her friendly smiled had vanished, but I recognized her porcelain skin and long brown hair. Her eyelids were closed, but it didn't make her dead body any easier to look at.

I slowly inched my way over to Meg, not really feeling my legs move beneath me. My fingers involuntarily reached out to take her limp hand. Agony twisted in my gut. It felt a lot like guilt, like her death and the carnage surrounding me was somehow my fault.

If I found Grace sooner... If I tried harder to get to her... If I explained things to Meg faster... Maybe all this could've been prevented.

I pushed Meg's hair out of her face. Her skin was still warm. I could almost pretend she was only sleeping.

The key we needed hung loosely around her neck. I leaned forward and undid the clasp. It didn't feel right claiming the key as my own, so instead of placing it around my neck, I slipped it into my pocket.

"Rest in peace, Meg," I whispered.

"Ryn." Someone placed a gentle hand on my shoulder, making me jump.

I turned to find Marek standing next to me. He'd retracted his wings, but he remained shirtless from the battle. Without thinking about it, I got to my feet and flung my hands around his neck. He gently wrapped me in his warm arms. Neither of us spoke. It was easier that way.

Minutes later, Fletcher approached us, and we were forced to part.

"How are we going to explain all this?" I asked, gesturing to the bodies lying in the grass nearby.

Fletcher's face fell. "This is going to be a terrible loss for the town. The Davina will all know what happened. As for everyone else... we'll have to explain it away as a mass accident."

"The demons will be back," Marek said quietly. It sounded as if speaking caused him pain.

"I know," Fletcher agreed. "We'll be contacting the Davina Council and bringing in as many Davina as we can. Everything will be easier once we wake Grace."

My stomach dropped. I couldn't explain the feeling in my gut that told me Grace wouldn't be able to fix this. Things would only get worse before this war was finally over.

END OF BOOK TWO

This story will continue in book three of the Divine Fate Trilogy, *Awakened by Grace.*

ABOUT THE AUTHOR

Alicia Rades is a USA Today bestselling author of young adult and new adult paranormal fiction. When she's not dreaming up magical stories, she's either binge-watching paranormal TV shows, meditating, or spending time with her family. She has an unhealthy obsession with psychic characters and writes with a deck of tarot cards next to her computer.

www.ingramcontent.com/pod-product-compliance
Lightning Source LLC
Chambersburg PA
CBHW031557310726
48974CB00003B/704